W9-CTX-265

MARTHA FREEMAN

CAMPFIRE COOKIES

A Paula Wiseman Book
Simon & Schuster Books for Young Readers
New York London Toronto Sydney New Delhi

Also by Martha Freeman

The Secret Cookie Club

SIMON & SCHUSTER BOOKS FOR YOUNG READERS
An imprint of Simon & Schuster Children's Publishing Division
1230 Avenue of the Americas, New York, New York 10020

Book design by Krista Vossen
The text for this book was set in Kepler Std.
Manufactured in the United States of America
0416 FFG
First Edition
2 4 6 8 10 9 7 5 3 1
Library of Congress Cataloging-in-Publication Data
Names: Freeman, Martha, 1956–
Title: Campfire cookies / Martha Freeman.
Description: New York : Simon & Schuster Books for Young Readers, [2016] |
Series: Secret Cookie Club ; [2] | "A Paula Wiseman Book." | Summary: "Secret Cookie Club members Grace, Emma, Olivia, and Lucy are thrilled to be back in Flowerpot Cabin with their beloved counselor, Hannah. But when a mysterious letter arrives, Hannah is plunged into despair. After puzzling out the contents of the letter, the campers make a plan to help Hannah—a plan that requires a daring mission to boys' camp and a big batch of campfire cookies."—Provided by publisher.
Identifiers: LCCN 2015029657| ISBN 9781481448215 (hardback) | ISBN 9781481448239 (eBook)
Subjects: | CYAC: Friendship—Fiction. | Camps—Fiction. | Cookies—Fiction. | Clubs—Fiction. |
BISAC: JUVENILE FICTION / Social Issues / Friendship.
| JUVENILE FICTION / Cooking & Food. | JUVENILE FICTION / Girls & Women.
Classification: LCC PZ7.F87496 Cai 2016 | DDC [Fic]—dc23
LC record available at http://lccn.loc.gov/2015029657

For my sister, Amy Boitano.
Both of us have good memories of summer camp in Arizona.
—M. A. F.

CHAPTER ONE

The scorpions, tarantulas, and rattlesnakes that live just outside the Moonlight Ranch main gate stay well out of the way on Camper Arrival Day, when the bare patch of ground they call home is overrun with human activity—cars pulling in and out, meetings and reunions, parents helping campers with heavy loads of luggage.

Scorpions, tarantulas, and rattlesnakes are shy and

peace-loving creatures. They want nothing to do with so much action.

While a few Moonlight Ranch campers always arrive on their own by shuttle from the Phoenix airport, most drive in with their parents. That late-June morning, families began arriving at ten, and by ten forty-five, Hannah Lehrer from Long Island, New York, was having second thoughts about her decision to come back for a second summer as counselor in Flowerpot Cabin.

Beside her stood the reason for those second thoughts, Olivia Baron, a tall, striking eleven-year-old black girl with drama queen tendencies and a scary-good vocabulary.

Hannah knew Olivia well. Hannah had been her counselor the year before and had greeted Olivia with a big hug when she alighted from the SUV her parents had rented for the drive. After that, the two had chatted eagerly about the summer to come.

"This year Flowerpot Cabin will totally dominate Chore Score!" Olivia announced. "Purple Sage is going down!"

Purple Sage was another ten-to-eleven girls cabin, and Chore Score, the daily measure of how thoroughly cabins were cleaned, was a big deal at Moonlight Ranch.

Hannah laughed. "My friend Jane's the counselor in Purple Sage again this year."

"What about the campers?" Olivia asked.

"One returning, the others new," said Hannah.

"I hope it's not that Brianna girl coming back," said Olivia. "She is *stuck-up*!"

"Come on, O. She's not that bad," said Hannah. "O" was Olivia's nickname.

"Oh, no-o-o!" Olivia moaned. "That means she *is* the one coming back! Is she here yet?"

"I don't think so," Hannah said. "Jane told me she's coming on one of the airport shuttles. Can I help you, Mrs. Baron? That crate looks heavy."

"It is! And thank you, Hannah." Together they hefted the crate up and onto a handcart already piled with Olivia's possessions. "What have you got in here, anyway, Livia?" her mom asked.

"That one?" Olivia studied it for a moment. "My backup iPad, my speakers, some batteries, some chargers, a game platform, controller, video monitor . . . and I think extra shoes."

Hannah's heart sank. "Uh, Olivia? Mrs. Baron? You know about the new no-electronics policy, right? You signed the contract. You must've."

"What's that mean—no electronics?" Olivia asked.

"Oh, dear," said Mrs. Baron. "My assistant sent in the paperwork. What is it that I missed?"

Anticipating that some parents might need a refresher on the policy, the camp director had given each counselor a copy of the letter describing it. Now Hannah pulled out the letter, unfolded it, and handed it to Olivia's mom.

Dear Moonlight Ranch families,

More than half a century ago, my parents established a sleepaway camp at their beautiful working cattle ranch in central Arizona. At first the camp was a modest affair, but over time it has grown into the nationally renowned operation that you know so well.

My own Moonlight Ranch journey began when I was a boy barely old enough to flake hay. I have seen many changes in the ensuing years, one of which brings me to my point in writing to you today. Recently, our highly qualified and caring professional staff has observed that our campers, like young people the world over, engage ever more frequently with their electronic devices.

The result, in too many cases, is that campers physically surrounded by our beautiful and expansive environment are mentally buried in the same restrictive screen experience they could have in their bedrooms at home.

For this reason, we at Moonlight Ranch have decided to declare camp property an electronics-free zone for the upcoming summer. No electronic devices of any kind, including cellular telephones, will be permitted. If parents need to get in touch with their campers, they may call Paula in the camp office anytime, day or night. Likewise, campers urgently needing to contact parents will have access to Paula around the clock.

In addition, all campers will be expected to write at least one letter home per week. In the same spirit, parents may wish to reciprocate by writing cards and letters to their campers.

To minimize misunderstanding and ensure that summer gets off to a smooth start, a contract outlining the no-electronics agreement is enclosed for your signature.

Thank you for your understanding, and we look forward to another rewarding summer for your sons and daughters here with our livestock in the wholesome Arizona desert.

Sincerely,

Jonathan S. "Buck" Cooper, Camp Director

P.S. As always, if you have any questions, please contact Paula in the camp office.

Olivia read over her mom's shoulder. As she did, her hand sought out the phone in the pocket of her shorts. By the time Mrs. Baron was done reading, Olivia was gripping her phone with white-knuckled devotion.

"I can't live without it!" she cried. "My friends will forget I exist!"

"Oh, darling. I am sorry," Mrs. Baron said. "I should have read this before. But don't you think it might be a nice idea to go a short while without all your gizmos? I wish I could give that a try."

This comment did not help matters. In fact, it catapulted Olivia into full-on drama queen mode. "A whole summer is *not* a *short while*!" she wailed. "You don't understand *anything*!"

It was then that Hannah questioned her decision to return to Moonlight Ranch.

To keep from saying something she'd regret, Hannah turned and looked across the desert. In her mind's eye, she saw the marble-lined corridors of the New York museum where she could have worked that summer, the dresses and high heels she'd be wearing, the weekends at the beach with her friends.

And she saw the best part of this parallel summer, her new boyfriend, Travis. He was the first real boyfriend she had ever had.

What am I doing out here in the middle of nowhere? she thought. *The sunshine is too bright. The air smells like dust and horses. My new jeans scratch, and my boots are heavy. My face feels sticky with sweat and sunscreen.*

To top it off, I'm arguing with an eleven-year-old!

Hannah sighed and mentally shook herself. This was the summer she had chosen. It was time to step up.

"Olivia?" She looked back at her camper. "During camp, your social life is here, and no one else has a phone either. Sorry, but you're going to have to leave that crate behind. And hand over your phone, too."

Slam! Olivia's dad closed the hatch of the SUV and turned to Hannah, smiling. "Whoa," he said, then, "Livia"—he looked at his daughter—"I think you might have met your match."

Olivia's dad was George Baron of Baron Barbecue Sauce, a staple on the shelves of every grocery store in

America. His and his wife's faces were even on the label. On the scale of Moonlight Ranch celebrities, the two of them were right up there with Brianna's mom, Natalya Silverbug, a former model who now sold a high-tech brand of dust mop on a shopping network.

Olivia folded her arms across her chest and set her jaw. She looked ready to do battle for her right to keep her phone. Then, all of a sudden, she backed down. "Oh, all right, fine." She pulled the phone from her pocket and handed it to her mom. "I guess I can live without it for one summer. It'll be good for me, right?"

Hannah wondered what had caused Olivia to change her mind so abruptly—but she was too grateful to say anything.

Mrs. Baron looked surprised too, but then recovered. "Exactly," she said, "and writing letters is fun. I'll send you some stickers to make them pretty, and some markers if you want. How would that be?"

"That would be cool, Mama," said Olivia. "Thank you."

Olivia's father shot Hannah a look that said thumbs-up. At the same time, a voice came from across the parking area. "Hannah! Over here!"

CHAPTER TWO

Hannah recognized the voice and wheeled around. "Emma!" she cried.

Olivia looked too, and here came Hannah's camper number two, Emma Rosen from Pennsylvania, jogging toward them. Halfway there she stepped on a loose rock and stumbled. *Uh-oh*, thought Hannah. *Off to the nurse already?*

But Emma stayed on her feet, kept moving, and kept smiling.

"Let me look at your hair! It's so long!" Olivia greeted her friend by tugging her brown wavy hair, pulled back with a bandanna—a style acceptable only at camp.

"*Too* long?" Emma asked.

"Yeah. No. It doesn't matter—I'm so excited to see you I could *die*!" Olivia grabbed Emma, and then both girls grabbed Hannah.

"Okay, okay." Hannah felt a little overwhelmed.

"Now you have to give over your phone," Olivia told Emma. "That's Buck's rule this summer. Can you believe it? I thought for sure I'd *die*!"

Hannah wasn't ready for another phone discussion. "Let's go say hi to your parents, Emma. Olivia, can you show your mom and dad the way to Flowerpot Cabin? I'll see you in the dining hall for lunch."

Olivia said, "I know the way to Flowerpot Cabin."

Emma grabbed Hannah's hand and tugged her across

the lot. Her parents—dad a doctor, mom a lawyer—were friendly but a little distracted, and as rumpled as Olivia's were glamorous. Hannah had just finished saying hello and pointing them toward Flowerpot Cabin when someone tapped her on her shoulder. She turned at the same time Emma squealed, *"Grace!"*

"Hello, Hannah. Hello, Emma. Have you noticed that it's awfully—" Grace Xi's question was stifled by Emma's big hug.

Looking at them, Hannah smiled. Her campers were delighted to see each other; didn't she deserve some credit for that? She was good at being a counselor. Maybe coming back this summer wasn't a mistake.

Last year the Flowerpot girls hadn't gotten along at first. Then, inspired by a dream about her late grandfather, Hannah had come up with the bright idea of having them make a batch of cookies one night after lights-out.

She had hoped the baking project would bring them together, and it had. In fact, they had all wanted to share Flowerpot Cabin again this summer.

"This way to Flowerpot Cabin." Hannah pointed for Emma and her parents. "And I'll see you in a few minutes in the dining hall. Come on, Grace. Your turn."

Grace was from Massachusetts, and her mom and dad both worked in high-tech firms near Boston. Mrs. Xi wore khakis, a white polo, and Top-Siders. Her light brown hair was pulled back with a headband.

Mr. Xi was Chinese, shorter than his wife and rounder, too. He had been born in Singapore, Hannah remembered. Last year Grace had gotten letters with foreign stamps.

Hannah shook hands with Mr. and Mrs. Xi and asked about their trip. Like most of the other families, they had flown into Phoenix the day before, spent the night in a hotel, and then rented a car for the ninety-mile drive northeast to Moonlight Ranch.

"You know where you're going?" Hannah asked for the third time that morning. "Flowerpot Cabin?"

"Grace will show us," said Mr. Xi.

Three down, one to go, thought Hannah, and she looked around for her last camper, Lucy Ambrose from

Beverly Hills, California. In the crowd, Hannah recognized a few young faces from the summer before and said hello, but there was no Lucy.

Should she worry? She knew Lucy's family was eccentric and—in spite of their fancy address—not as well-off as most of the others who sent campers to Moonlight Ranch. She also remembered that Lucy's mom's outfit—green short shorts with red cowboy boots—had caused a stir at the farewell lunch last year.

But none of that explained why Lucy was late.

At Moonlight Ranch there are fifty cabins laid out behind split-rail fences on either side of a dirt road—girls' cabins to the right, boys' to the left. The dining hall and kitchen are near the entrance gate. The pond, horse barn, playing fields, show ring, campfire pit, and outbuildings are over a hill where the road dead-ends.

Beyond that, cattle graze, each one bearing the Moonlight Ranch laughing moon brand on its flank.

At lunch the Xi, Baron, and Rosen families sat around

a long table, ate sandwiches and drank milk, chocolate milk, or iced tea.

"I'm sure the summer will pass quickly," said Mr. Baron. "In fact, it doesn't seem so long ago that we were all here together. But aren't we missing someone?"

"Are we?" Dr. Rosen looked around.

"Yes, honey. We're missing Lucy," said Mrs. Rosen.

"*And* Vivek," said Olivia, looking at Grace.

Mr. Xi looked at his daughter. "Who's Vivek?"

When Grace didn't answer, Hannah said, "I remember Vivek. He was in Lasso Cabin. I think I saw his name on the list for this summer. Do you guys know for sure if he's coming back?"

"He wrote to Lucy after the coyote and everything," Emma said. "So yeah, he's coming back. But I haven't seen him."

Olivia looked around. "Me neither. Have you seen him, Grace?"

"Come on, O, give her a break!" said Emma.

Olivia grinned, and Hannah remembered something about Grace having a crush on Vivek. To help her out, she changed the subject. "Wasn't that awesome about Lucy and the coyote?" Hannah asked. "Did you all hear that story?"

"Oh, yes, but I don't think I learned the details. Can you remind us?" asked Mrs. Xi.

Olivia said, "I can! What happened was a *really, really, really* huge wolf with *really, really, really, really* long teeth was getting ready to ambush a chubby little boy Lucy babysits so—*pow!*—Lucy kicked a soccer ball and nailed it, and it was half dead but slunk off into the underbrush. Meanwhile, the little boy was *totally* fine, not eaten at all, and afterward Lucy was on TV because she was a hero!"

"It was a coyote," said Grace.

Olivia shrugged. "Same thing."

Emma said, "The point is that Lucy's a hero."

Olivia asked, "Where is she, anyway, Hannah?"

"She'll be here soon," said Hannah, hoping she was right.

While the campers and their families ate, Buck had been making the rounds. Now he came to Hannah's table. "Welcome back. Welcome back. It's a pleasure to have you girls here again. Flowerpot Cabin, I think?"

"It's the *best* cabin in the whole camp!" said Olivia.

Buck smiled. "Well, I don't know about that. But I'm sure glad you think so. Hannah," he went on, "I count one, two, three campers. Are we missing somebody?"

"Lucy Ambrose," said Hannah.

Buck frowned. "I'd better look into that. Excuse me, won't you? Good to see you all."

When lunch was over, it was time for the parents to leave. The three families trekked out of the dining hall down the path and under the Moonlight Ranch entrance gate, which was topped with a rendering of the laughing moon brand, and back to the makeshift parking lot. In central camp, there were cottonwood trees for shade, but out here the midday sun blazed full force, turning parked cars into solar ovens.

To give the families space for their good-byes, Hannah walked a few paces behind. She was feeling better about her decision to return to camp. Like the other counselors, she had arrived four days earlier for O & T—orientation and training. Up till now it had been nice to have Flowerpot Cabin to herself, to fall asleep to the songs of owls and crickets.

But she didn't think it would be so bad to fall asleep to the sounds of girls giggling and whispering. She had missed them.

Hannah gave herself a pep talk: It was going to be a good summer.

Even though she would learn absolutely nothing about art.

Even though she'd never once get to the beach.

Even though she missed Travis a whole lot already.

It was going to be a good—

Wait. What was that noise? Was she imagining it? It was something from the city, not something you expected at camp.

She looked around . . . and realized she wasn't crazy. Other people heard the noise too.

But what was a siren doing in the middle of the Arizona desert?

CHAPTER THREE

Along with everybody else, Hannah turned to look in the direction of the siren—down the gravel drive that led to the state highway half a mile away.

Soon she saw what looked like a puff of dust illuminated by flashes of red and blue. . . . The puff of dust became a smudge shimmering in the heat. . . . The shimmering smudge became a white police cruiser, moving fast, its lights whirling, siren blaring.

About fifty yards out, the driver must've let up on the gas, because the cruiser slowed, until finally, just as it reached the entrance to the dirt lot, it rolled to a stop. At the same time, the sound of the siren dropped in pitch and volume from shriek to moan to sigh and then, finally, silence.

The blue-and-red lights went dark. The cruiser sat. The assembled parents, campers, and counselors watched and waited. Nobody said a word.

Then came the *click-thunk* of a latch, and the back passenger door opened, and a petite girl with a snub nose and tousled blond hair climbed out, yawned, blinked twice, and looked around.

"I guess I fell asleep," she said.

"Lucy-y-y-y!" Olivia cried. And all in a rush, she and Emma and Grace ran toward the car. Soon they had half smothered their friend in a group hug. At the same time, Lucy's mom alighted from the front passenger seat, and after her, the trooper who'd been driving climbed out too.

By this time, Buck had hustled over from the camp

office. Speaking to the trooper, he kept his voice low, but Hannah could see he was pretty revved up—red-faced and gesturing broadly.

"Lucy, how are you?" Hannah said. "Girls, give her some air! Hello, Mrs. Ambrose. I'm Hannah, Lucy's counselor—remember? Great to see you. I hope everything is okay."

"Oh, Hannah—yes, of course." Lucy's mom had a movie-star shape and a movie-star smile. At least, Hannah thought, she was dressed perfectly normally that day in capris, a T-shirt, and sneakers. "What a nightmare!" she said. "But now we're fine, aren't we, Lucy? Thank merciful heaven for kind Officer Leonard here. What would we have done without him?"

"I'm really sorry," said Hannah. "It must've been terrible. But what exactly happened?"

Lucy's mom shook her head and then looked at the sky as if she were looking at God. "What *didn't* happen?" she replied.

Hannah waited a second for more, but that seemed to be it. "Well, okay then," Hannah said. "Do you have Lucy's stuff for her? We should grab that for move-in and—"

"Yes, yes. Go ahead," said Lucy's mom. "Officer Leonard? Excuse me? Hello, Mr. Cooper. I'm Karen Kathleen Ambrose—KK for short. Yes, I thought you'd remember me. It's thrilling to be here at last, let me tell you. Could I borrow Officer Leonard? Just to get Lucy's things from the trunk?"

The next few minutes were hectic as Grace, Emma, and Olivia tried simultaneously to say good-bye to their parents and hello to Lucy and her mom. Eventually, Emma's, Olivia's, and Grace's parents all drove off, waving.

As for Lucy, she gave her mom a hug that was more dutiful than affectionate, and then her mom left the same way she had arrived, minus the lights and sirens.

With some help from Buck, Hannah and the girls hauled Lucy's stuff to Flowerpot Cabin. In the doorway, Buck said, "Everything good here? Lucy? You good?"

Lucy was kneeling on the floor by her footlocker, studying one of the latches.

"Lucy!" Emma got her attention. "Mr. Cooper is talking to you."

"What?" Lucy looked at Emma, then at Buck. "Oh! I'm well, Mr. Cooper. How are you?"

Olivia cracked up and then Grace did, too. Buck said, "I'm fine too, Lucy. So, I, uh, guess I'll leave you girls to settle in."

Buck generally wore a big ivory-colored cowboy hat around camp, a hat that would have looked silly on anyone else but looked practical on him, the same as his boots and jeans. Now he touched the brim of the hat and ducked through the doorway and out onto the flagstone walk that wound among all the girls' cabins.

Hannah followed. "Buck," she said, "excuse me, I was wondering, uh . . . is there anything I should know about what's going on with Lucy? The police and everything?"

Buck said, "Car broke down and no cell phone. I'm no fan of the things, but they are handy for emergencies. Anyway, somebody called in the car on the side of the highway, and the troopers responded."

"What about the siren?" said Hannah.

"That seems to have resulted from *somebody's* flare for the dramatic," Buck said.

"Lucy's mom, you mean?"

Buck nodded. "I chewed the officer out. To my way of thinking, that's no reason to alarm the herd. I'm confident that next time Officer Leonard will think twice before offering sound effects as a public service."

CHAPTER FOUR

By the time Hannah returned to Flowerpot Cabin, Lucy's flashy arrival was old news. Instead, the conversation was all about the other missing camper, Vivek.

Hannah tried to remember what she knew about Vivek. He was a handsome kid with long eyelashes. Also, by sheer coincidence, he had been in the camp kitchen the night last summer when she had organized cookie baking for her girls.

Hannah believed in respecting her campers' privacy and tried not to listen in on their chatter. This was hard when they were confined in the small cabin together.

"We're sure Vivek is going to be here this year, right?" Grace said.

"I thought he e-mailed you," Emma said.

"Yes, but something might've gone wrong after," Grace said.

"Why would any of us know that?" asked Emma.

"I haven't seen Vivek," said Olivia. "But I'll tell you who I *have* seen. That new counselor, Lance. OMG, what a hunk he is!"

Hannah was seated at the cabin's only desk, sorting through camper arrival paperwork. She was in a hurry. It had to be turned in to Paula in the office by five. Still, she couldn't help laughing. "Don't you think Lance is just a little old for you?"

"He's probably twenty-one, right?" Olivia said. "So when I'm twenty-one, he'll be thirty-one."

"But you're not twenty-one *now*," said Emma, always the sensible one. "And by the time you are, you won't be interested in Lance. You won't even know him anymore."

"Still," said Grace, "there is nothing wrong with looking, is there?"

"Grace!" said Emma. "I can't believe you said that!"

Grace giggled. "I can't believe I did either."

"Well I, for one, appreciate your comment, Grace," said Olivia. "Lucy, what are you doing down there on the floor?"

Lucy responded without looking up. "Lance is in Silver Spur Cabin."

"How do you know?" Olivia asked.

"I didn't think she was even listening," said Grace.

"I remembered because his name is medieval," said Lucy.

"Wait, *what*?" Olivia asked.

Now Lucy looked up from her footlocker, which still wouldn't open. "You know, like they had jousting matches back in King Arthur's time," she said. "And they jousted with *lances*."

"But how did you know what cabin he's in?" Olivia persisted. "You just got here."

Lucy didn't answer. She had gone back to the problem of opening her footlocker.

Grace said, "Lance *is* handsome. He looks like Ryan Gosling only decades younger."

"But he's not as handsome as Vive-e-ek," Olivia teased.

Grace blew out her cheeks. "Am I going to have to put up with this all summer?"

"Yes," said Olivia. "But it's okay because we're all members of the Secret Cookie Club!"

"To the membership!" Emma raised her fists and grinned.

"To the membership!" Grace raised her fists but did not grin. "I hate unpacking," she said. "I hate when everything's disorganized."

Hannah looked up from her paperwork. Grace's bunk, she saw, was already made-up with a new pink-and-blue checkered quilt. On top, Grace's clothes were laid out in neatly folded piles—on their way to their final destination, Grace's bureau.

Nothing about her was disorganized.

Emma was looking at Grace's bunk too. "OMG, you're

like my mother!" Emma said. "You sort your socks by color!"

Grace said, "Most people do that. Don't they?"

"No," said Olivia.

"No," said Emma.

Lucy didn't say anything.

"Did you lose the key, Lu?" Emma asked her.

No answer.

Olivia said, "That's solid concentration there."

"We could try kicking her," Grace said.

"Grace!" Emma protested.

"I mean gently," said Grace.

"You don't have to kick me," said Lucy.

"She speaks!" said Olivia.

"There is no key anymore," Lucy said. "It should just open when you move this slide thing over, only the slide thing won't move."

Emma knelt to inspect the situation. "I think maybe the spring's stuck. See?"

"This," said Olivia, "is why God invented camp counselors. Hannah! We need you!"

Hannah mimed, "Who, me?" then laid down her pen and crossed the room to inspect Lucy's footlocker. It was dented. The metal parts were rust-stained and askew.

"Lucy, my friend," she said, "no offense, but that trunk is not worth saving. Is it okay if we use my trusty hammer? We can pry the latch open with it or—worst case—bust it."

Lucy said, "It was my grandpa's. He was a soldier."

"Wow—it's historic!" said Emma. "We can't just bust it."

Lucy shrugged. "So I'll wear the same T-shirt and shorts all summer."

Olivia looked Lucy up and down. "That would be a mistake," she said.

"And what about your underwear?" Grace asked.

"Yeah, underwear—*hello-o-o-o*?" said Olivia.

"Vivek is in Silver Spur Cabin this summer," said Lucy. "That's how I know that Lance is the counselor there."

"Wait, *what*?" Olivia looked around. "Can everyone else keep up with her all the time?"

"Hannah's hammer made me think of a weapon, and

that made me think of 'lance'—small 'l,' which made me think of 'Lance'—big 'l,' which made me think of Vivek again," said Lucy. "Hannah, it's okay if you get your hammer to open the footlocker. Till we started looking around, my nana didn't even know she still had it. So let's just pretend it still doesn't exist."

Hannah said okay—even though she didn't exactly understand what Lucy had said. "We've got stuff to do before dinner, you guys. You all need to finish unpacking."

While Hannah looked for her hammer, Grace asked, "Can we go back to the Vivek part?"

"Vivek told me he was in Silver Spur Cabin," said Lucy.

"The plot thickens!" said Olivia.

"*When* did he tell you?" Grace asked.

"Last week when he called me," said Lucy.

"He called you at your *house*?" said Grace.

Lucy looked at Olivia. "Didn't I just say that?"

"Yes," said Olivia.

Emma tried to explain. "Lucy, Grace is surprised because—"

Grace cut Emma off. "What *else* did Vivek say when he called you at your house?"

Lucy looked from Emma to Grace and back. "Uh . . . his parents are supposed to go to India this summer. He thinks I'm brave for fighting a wild animal." She shrugged. "That's about it."

"So do you know where he is now?" Grace asked.

"Silver Spur Cabin?" Lucy said.

"No, he's not!" Grace said. "He isn't here yet. Nobody's seen him."

"Weird," said Lucy.

"Here you go." Hannah had found the hammer, which was pink. She handed it to Lucy and told her she could use the flat end to pry the footlocker open.

Lucy didn't listen. In one motion, she took the hammer and swung it hard.

Thwack—the latch sprang, and the lid popped up like someone startled awake.

Lucy grinned. "*That* was satisfying." She handed Hannah back her hammer and started to unpack.

CHAPTER FIVE

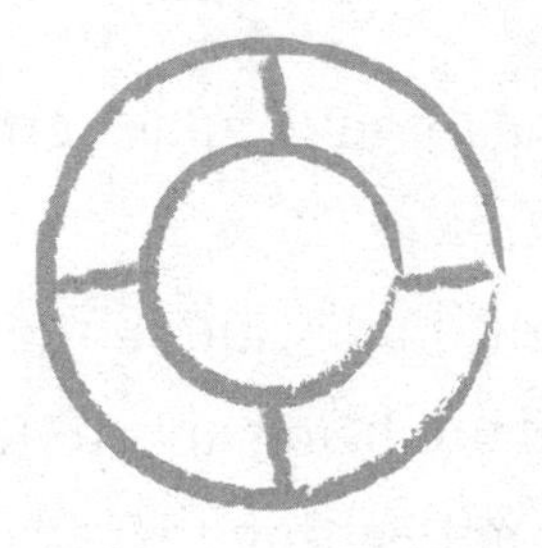

An hour later, the girls of Flowerpot Cabin had put away their stuff, and Hannah had gathered them to sit in a circle on the varnished red-clay floor. In the middle of the circle lay construction paper, drawing paper, four pairs of scissors, a new box of markers, and glue.

"Okay, so you know we have the whole no-electronics thing?" Hannah began.

Olivia put her hand to her heart and moaned, "Don't remind me!"

"I keep reaching for my phone," Emma said.

"Me too," said Grace.

"Oh, it's not that bad." Hannah was getting used to it. True, she hated not being able to text Travis, and she hated even more not getting texts from Travis. But she liked writing him postcards—four, so far, which she granted might be excessive. Anyway, he had promised to write her back.

"So the point is no electronics is not the only new thing," Hannah said. "Another one is this team-building activity."

Different as they were, Grace, Emma, Olivia, and Lucy agreed on one thing. They hated team-building activities: *"No-o-o-o!"* they chorused.

Hannah pressed on. "Tonight at the campfire," she said, "all the cabins have to present what they've done, and then we get s'mores. So this is a step on the road to s'mores. Okay?"

"Do you get in trouble if we don't do it?" Emma asked.

"We didn't do have to do team-building last summer," said Olivia.

"Do we get points?" Grace asked.

"Do we get to draw?" Lucy asked.

"The points count for Top Cabin," Hannah said. "And yes, you *do* get to draw. The idea is we're making flags, one for each of you first and then one for Flowerpot Cabin, for all of us. That one they're going to hang in the dining hall with everybody else's, like pennants. Your own personal flag represents stuff that's important to you, so we get to know each other better."

"We already know each other," said Olivia. "This is stupid."

Emma said, "That's not very nice, O."

Olivia clarified. "I didn't say Hannah was stupid, just her activity."

"We get points," Grace reminded them.

"Can we just do this?" Hannah said.

"Sure. What's the holdup?" Olivia said.

It was quiet for a while after that except for the soft scratching of marker on paper. Then Olivia announced her flag was done, and soon after her, Lucy and then Emma.

"Okay, so who's ready to tell what you drew?" Hannah asked.

Grace said, "I'm not done yet."

Olivia looked over at Grace's paper. "Are those supposed to be waves, Grace? Everything's so tiny I can't tell."

Grace sat back and shook out her right hand. "It's the ocean," she said. "And these are skyscrapers."

Lucy said, "It's really good. Lots of details."

"Do you want to tell us what you drew, Grace?" Hannah asked.

Grace explained that she had drawn skyscrapers in two cities, Singapore, where her dad was from and his family still lived, and Boston, where her mom was from. She had also drawn a ballet slipper because she took ballet lessons, a piano because she took piano lessons, and a test tube because she liked science.

"And here"—she pointed—"is a plate of cookies because we all like cookies."

On Emma's drawing was a Star of David because she was Jewish and a picture of two little boys, one white wearing ice skates and one black. The white one was her brother, Benjamin. The other was a kid named Kayden whom she tutored in reading after school.

"What are the musical notes for?" Grace asked.

"He likes to dance," said Emma. "He even makes me dance with him in the hall outside the library."

"That must be funny," said Olivia.

Emma said, "It is. Oh, and I drew cookies too."

Lucy's picture had kids too, little ones—the triplets whom she babysat. Their names were Arlo, Mia, and Levi.

"Which one did you save from the big bad wolf?" Olivia asked.

"It was a coyote," said Grace.

"You should let Lucy tell," said Olivia.

"It was a coyote," said Lucy.

"Same thing," said Olivia. "And I think you should've drawn a wolf in your picture too, Lucy. It would have added *drama*."

"I drew cookies like Emma did," Lucy said, "and a soccer ball."

"I hope you're not going to be stuck-up about how you're a hero now and everything," Olivia said.

"Olivia?" Hannah raised her eyebrows.

"That wasn't rude. It was honest," Olivia said. "People do get stuck-up sometimes. Like my brother. He plays baseball, and he is conceited. Anyway, do you want to hear about my flag? Or maybe nobody cares"—she sighed—"about little old me."

"Go ahead, Olivia," said Hannah.

Olivia's drawing took up the whole page. On it was a pink-lipped princess with a gold crown and gold earrings. Next to one ear was a phone. "The princess is for when I played the princess in *The Princess and the Pea*," she explained. "And the phone is because I miss my phone. Oh—and I drew cookies, chocolate like the ones Emma sent me."

Hannah looked at Emma. "Did you use my grandfather's recipe?"

"I did," Emma said.

"Wait, Emma, *shhhh*! That's supposed to be a secret!" said Grace.

"What's a secret?" Hannah asked.

"The Secret Cookie Club," said Lucy.

Grace slapped her head. *"Lucy!"*

Hannah couldn't help laughing. "To be honest, you guys, I kind of knew already. I mean, I was there when you planned it."

"You were asleep," Grace said.

"Not totally," said Hannah. "Did you really send each other cookies all year?"

"Letters and homemade cookies that we made from your grandfather's recipes, Hannah, the ones you gave us the last day of camp," Emma said. "And you know what? Flour power works!"

Flour power was Hannah's grandfather's idea that homemade baked goods could fix most problems.

Emma looked around at Lucy, Olivia, and Grace. "I think I know what we should put on the Flowerpot Cabin flag to take to the campfire tonight," she said.

"A flowerpot?" Lucy said.

"No, not a flowerpot," Grace said. *"Cookies!"*

"Duh," said Olivia.

"Oh, I see," said Lucy. "Can I draw it? I like to draw, and I won a ribbon for art this year."

"Ha!" said Olivia. "I knew it! You *are* getting stuck-up."

"Give her a break, O. What she's saying is obvious," said Emma. "Look at our drawings and look at hers."

Emma was right. Each triplet's distinct personality came out in Lucy's drawings, and the soccer ball looked ready to bounce off the page.

Without her phone, Hannah was wearing a plain, old-fashioned watch. Now she checked it and said, "Almost dinnertime, girls. We have to get a move on."

"No wonder I'm starving!" said Olivia. "Hurry up and draw our cookie flag, Lucy. Then we can go eat."

CHAPTER SIX

Vivek was not at dinner.

But a tall girl with terrific posture was. She had shoulder-length, straight black hair and perfectly arched eyebrows in a round face with a strong, determined chin. Her clothes were obviously expensive.

She was Brianna Silverbug.

Of the Flowerpot girls, Olivia noticed her first and immediately narrowed her eyes. Before Olivia could say anything, Hannah did: "You guys, let's go meet the Purple Sage girls. You're the same age group, and our cabins are on the same walkway. You ought to get to know each other."

Besides Brianna, the Purple Sage campers were Kate, Maria, and Haley. Jane, the Purple Sage counselor, knew everyone in Flowerpot from the summer before, and while they were all in line at the salad bar she made introductions. The smiles, hellos, and where're-you-froms were shy but friendly, Hannah thought, except between Brianna and Olivia. Those two barely spoke.

Later, when it was time to go up to the campfire, Hannah and Jane walked together. "What is up between my Olivia and your Brianna, anyway?" Hannah asked in a low voice. "Do you know?"

Jane looked around to make sure none of the campers was listening. "I don't. But something must've happened last year. I expected hissing and snarling any second."

"I barely know Brianna. What's she like?" Hannah said.

"She's great. Smart, funny, works hard. Super

competent on a horse too," Jane said. "She's one of the ones who gets to bring her own to camp. Maybe she's a little, uh . . . inflexible? She gets an idea in her head and it's hard to talk her out of it."

Hannah nodded. "That last part sounds like Olivia, so that could be the problem. They're a little too similar."

"Maybe," Jane said. "Anyway, we super mature counselors better monitor the situation if we don't want all-out war. Oh, and did I mention another good thing about Brianna? She brought us a Dandy Dust Mop."

"Seriously?" Hannah recalled seeing Brianna's mom on TV. "The only mop with patented dandy dust action?"

"'When it comes to dust, Dandy dominates,'" Jane quoted. "And that means when it comes to Chore Score, Purple Sage is gonna dominate too!"

"Dream on, Jane, my friend," said Hannah. "Even with your fancy electric dust mop, you guys can't possibly win. My girls are exceptionally tidy. Grace even sorts her socks by color."

Jane made a face. "*That's* just weird. And anyway, the

Chore Score has nothing to do with sock sorting. It's not even a category."

The walk from central camp to the campfire pit was all uphill. It had been full daylight when everyone started out, but by now the sun had set and a few stars were winking into view. All told, there were some two hundred campers at Moonlight Ranch that year, along with fifty counselors and half a dozen other staff. With everyone there at once, it was a mob scene, and it took Jane and Hannah several minutes to find their girls and shepherd them to their places.

(From the Moonlight Ranch Handbook for Families)

Among the many time-honored traditions at Moonlight Ranch, Campfire may be the most beloved. Several times each summer, the close-knit camp community gathers at the campfire pit just as dusk settles a splendid lilac cloak upon the desert. Comfortably seated on rustic, hand-hewn logs, campers, counselors, and staff enjoy the spectacle of the cheery campfire flames as they spring to life.

Of course, proper safety precautions are rigidly followed at all times, and we at Moonlight Ranch can point with pride to a safety record almost entirely unblemished.

Accompanied by the strumming of a talented counselor's guitar, campers join in a singalong of traditional American classics, such as "Oh! Susanna," "Red River Valley," and "She'll Be Comin' 'Round the Mountain."

The musical interlude concluded, information vital to community well-being and harmony are imparted during announcements. As necessary or desirable, additional programmatic elements are added.

At the Welcome Campfire, which concludes Camper Arrival Day, each counselor rises in turn to introduce the campers in his or her cabin. At the Farewell Campfire, Moonlight Ranch's coveted awards for Chore Score and Top Cabin are bestowed.

Every Moonlight Ranch Campfire concludes with the

enjoyment of a traditional culinary treat, the s'more. Half a lifetime's experience in recreation management has taught Moonlight Ranch director John S. "Buck" Cooper this valuable lesson: The maximum number of people who can safely and effectively roast marshmallows around a campfire is twenty.

Because the Moonlight Ranch community includes almost ten times that number, our s'mores are premade in the camp kitchen, using graham crackers as well as a nutritious and tasty combination of Marshmallow Fluff and chocolate frosting. For accommodation of your son's or daughter's special dietary needs, please contact Paula in the camp office.

During O & T, Annie, the head counselor, had encouraged everyone to speak clearly but quickly. Otherwise the introductions would go on all night. Waiting for her turn, Hannah felt the fire's heat on her cheeks. She hated public speaking, but inevitably her turn came, and she stood up.

"Hi. I'm Hannah from New York! I live in Flowerpot

Cabin with Grace, Emma, Olivia, and Lucy, and all of us like cookies!" On cue, the girls held up the cookie flag. A few people laughed; a few applauded. Someone called out, "Where's the cookies?"

Relieved to be done, Hannah dropped back onto her log, and Sharif, the counselor from Cactus Cabin, jumped up to take his turn.

"You did fine," Emma whispered to Hannah.

"Only your knees were knocking," said Olivia.

"Shhh!" Grace leaned over. "We'll get demerits!"

By this time, Sharif was sitting down. Hannah hadn't heard a word he said, but the drawing on his flag looked like a piece of rope with eyes. A rattlesnake, maybe?

Meanwhile, Lance, well-known hunk, got to his feet. "My boys are Jamil, Luke, Zach, and Vivek," he said. "We are Silver Spur Cabin, and our flag"—he held up a drawing of a black blob with eight black legs—"is a tarantula!"

The Silver Spur boys thought they were hilarious . . . till it came time for Blazing Star Cabin to introduce themselves, and they had a tarantula flag too.

Meanwhile, Olivia said, "Lance is *so dreamy.* Isn't he dreamy?"

Emma kicked her. "Shhh!"

Olivia said, "Don't you think he's dreamy, Hannah?"

Hannah echoed Emma. "Shhh!" But in truth she agreed that Lance, with his blond hair and green eyes, was handsome.

Not that she cared. She was interested in only one boy and one boy only, the one back home, Travis.

Grace leaned over. "Where's Vivek?" she whispered. "Lance *said* Vivek, but there is no Vivek."

"*Shhh!*" said Olivia.

"I'll ask him after the campfire," Hannah whispered just as Jane stood up to introduce the Purple Sage girls. ". . . and our flag is purple sage!" she said, displaying a drawing of gray-green leaves and a giant stalk of purple flowers.

"Oh, wow, how *original*," said Olivia.

"*Shhh!*" said Emma.

The last counselor on his feet was Jack from Yucca Cabin (boys fourteen to sixteen). The older boys were notoriously hard on counselors, and Jack was the first in a decade to come back for a second summer.

Hannah didn't know what to make of Jack. He was different from the other guys at Moonlight Ranch, and not remotely a hunk. He was a little overweight, for one thing, and he routinely made some peculiar wardrobe choices. For example, most of the guys wore sneakers, Tevas, or Western boots, but unless he was actually on horseback, Jack wore either Toms or flip-flops. As for his head, most guys wore cowboy hats or ball caps, while Jack favored the kind of small-brimmed hat with a hat-band that Hannah associated with old men in Florida.

Now Jack stood up, brushed campfire schmutz off his jeans, and said, "Nice to meet you, everybody. I'm Jack from Chicago, and these are my campers Simon, Jake, Kane, and Mitch—and *we are Yucca Cabin*!"

Jack held up their flag with a flourish, causing the four campers beside him to laugh uncontrollably . . . and everyone else either to hoot or to groan. The drawing showed a lumpy pattern of brown circles tinged with grass green. It wasn't especially realistic, but it was so familiar as to be unmistakable: horse poop.

Buck shook his head. "*That* will look nice in the dining hall."

"Won't it?" Jack grinned.

"You may sit down now," said Buck.

"Yes, sir," said Jack.

The Welcome Campfire was almost over. Annie, the head counselor, rose to make announcements about the next day's schedule as plastic-wrapped s'mores were handed out.

"My campers want to know about mail," a counselor said. "Some of them seem to be going a little bonkers without their phones."

Annie gestured toward a tired-looking woman with short gray hair and glasses who had been standing on the periphery of the campfire circle. "Paula?" she said. "Do you want to address that?"

Paula's expression said no, she did not, but now that she was on the spot, she stepped forward. "The mail gets here before noon," she said. "I should have it sorted in time to get you your letters at lunchtime. Oh, and while I'm here, I'll go ahead and remind you that your first letters home are due Sunday before dinner."

Paula retreated, and Buck stepped forward. "I know you're all wondering about scoring for your flags—am I right?" he said.

Most of the girls clapped and said, *"Ye-e-es!"* while the boys hooted and hollered, or, in the case of Yucca Cabin, answered, *"No-o-o!"*

"Flags are worth a possible three points toward the Top Cabin score," Buck explained, "and I'm pleased to announce that most cabins earned all three points. The exceptions are Cactus Cabin, whose rattlesnake looks like no rattlesnake this ol' cowboy has ever seen, and Yucca Cabin, who apparently did not buy into the proper spirit of the exercise."

Apparently the Yucca fourteen to sixteens appreciated being singled out because they now cheered wildly for their failure.

Meanwhile, Buck wished everybody a great summer

and a good night. "Counselors?" he said. "Lights-out in thirty minutes, no exceptions."

Hannah had not even had the chance to lift her rear end from its resting place when Grace leaned over. "Go ask Lance about Vivek. You said you would."

"Okay," Hannah said. "But is it okay with you if I eat the last s'more crumbs first?"

"I guess so," Grace said reluctantly . . . then she must have realized she was being rude. "I'm sorry, Hannah. I meant to say 'please.' *Please*?"

Hannah smiled. She'd had her share of crushes too. "It's okay," she said. "I see Lance over there."

In the crowd of campers and counselors headed back to central camp, Lance's three were in a huddle, which he followed like a sheepdog. Hannah walked fast to catch up. "Hey, hi, uh, excuse me?" she said. Lance was new this year, and the two had barely spoken during O & T. "I'm Hannah."

"Flowerpot Cabin, I know," Lance said. "The one with the celebrities."

"Celebrities?" Hannah repeated.

"The barbecue heiress," said Lance. "The coyote killer."

"Is that how people think of my campers?" Hannah shook her head. "I'd rather they thought of what's on our flag—you know, cookies."

"Uh-oh. I hope they don't think of us as *our* flag," said Lance.

Hannah wrinkled her nose. "Yeah, tarantula."

"Like every other boys' cabin," Lance said. "Maybe I shouldn't have talked them out of saddle sore."

Hannah laughed and Lance did, too. He had a nice smile, and his green eyes seemed more interesting than her own blue ones.

"Look." Hannah got to the point. "One of your campers, Vivek. My girls are asking where he is."

"Oh, yeah?" Lance said. "Is he some kind of preteen heartthrob?"

Hannah let that question go. "They know him from last summer. Is he okay?"

"I don't know exactly," said Lance. "Maybe don't tell your campers this, but Paula in the office said family emergency. I guess it's not too bad, because he's supposed to be here soon."

Hannah was puzzled. "Is there such a thing as a not-too-bad emergency?"

Lance shrugged. "Details to come. Okay, you knuckleheads"—he said this to his boys—"we go thataway, remember?" They were back in central camp by now, boys' cabins to their right, girls' to their left.

"Thanks for the info," Hannah said.

"Sure," said Lance. "Oh, hey—I've got evening riding. How about you?"

"Evening too," said Hannah.

"That's cool," he said. "I guess—" But she would never find out what he guessed because one of his campers grabbed his arm. "Come *on,* Lance!"

"Yeah, say good night to your *girl*friend," said another one.

Rolling his eyes, Lance allowed himself to be pulled away. "*Real* mature," he said to Hannah, who shrugged.

"That's boys for you," she said.

CHAPTER SEVEN

Grace

It took Hannah forever to get back from the campfire. When she did, I was waiting for her right inside the Flowerpot Cabin door. "What did Lance say?"

"Grace!" Hannah jumped. "You startled me!"

"Sorry," I said. "What did Lance say? Where's Vivek?"

Hannah took a breath. "He said there's nothing to worry about. He said there was some kind of a, uh . . . delay. Vivek will be here soon."

If you ask me, this sounded suspicious, and I was ready with another question . . . but stopped. Hannah was giving me a certain look I knew well. It was the same look my teacher Mrs. Keeran gave me the time I went up to her desk after school to argue about getting a ninety-nine instead of one hundred on the "Rip Van Winkle" book report.

The look meant: "Further discussion will not be productive."

"Your turn, Grace!" Emma came out of the bathroom.

"Okay, Emma, thanks," I said, and five minutes later I was climbing into my nice clean bed and hoping the other girls would not be noisy and keep me awake.

Don't get me wrong, I love Emma, Olivia, and Lucy.

Along with Shoshi Rubinstein at home in Massachusetts, they are my best friends in the whole world.

But a person doesn't always want to stay up talking. A person sometimes is tired.

My bunkmates must have been tired too, because I heard very little giggling before the sounds of even breathing won out. Still, I could not allow myself to fall asleep immediately. I had worrying to do.

First, there was Vivek. I do not have a crush on him the way the other girls think I do. I *do not!* Vivek is just a nice, handsome boy like any other nice, handsome boy who is also polite and smart and funny. Also, I think he is actually my friend. I don't have that many friends who are boys. In fact, he is the only one. I would like to keep him.

Also, I won't lie. I had been very surprised when Lucy said that she had talked to Vivek on the phone. Why would Vivek have called Lucy?

I mean, it is perfectly okay that he called Lucy. It is a free country. Vivek may call anyone he wants. But why would he call Lucy? He has never called me.

I had asked Lucy this question earlier that evening, when we were walking to dinner. I had chosen a moment when no one else could hear, so no one else (Olivia) would tease me. I was pretty sure Lucy would not tease me. I was pretty sure I could have a crush on SpongeBob, or Oz the great and powerful, or a giraffe at the zoo, and Lucy would not tease me. She would not even notice.

Apparently, Lucy notices wild animals that threaten triplets. Other than that, she mostly sees what is going on in her own head.

"He called to ask if I had sent him cookies," Lucy said.

"*Did* you send him cookies?" I asked.

"Yes," said Lucy. "Did you?"

"Yes," I said.

"Me too," said Emma, coming up behind us.

"So did O," said Lucy. "At least, I think she did, because Vivek said he got four boxes of cookies, each at a different time, and one was from Kansas City." Lucy giggled. "He sounded pretty confused."

There are several things you have to get used to if you are going to be happy at Moonlight Ranch. One is heat. One is your sore thighs and rear end from riding a horse every day. And one is the sound of the bell.

The bell I mean is not electronic. It is a real bell attached to a rope and hanging at the top of a wood tower in front of the dining hall. A live person rings it. The sound is clear and musical and loud.

The bell rings to announce the start of activities. It rings to announce meals. It rings to say lights-out, and most importantly, it rings to announce wake-up, which is at six forty-five.

Some people (Olivia) complain all summer long that this is too early, but I am used to getting up early. If you do not get up early, how are you supposed to get everything done?

At camp that first morning, Monday, I woke up before the bell and automatically reached for my phone.

Then I remembered.

So while I waited for the bell to ring, I worried about Vivek. What did "soon" mean anyway?

I worried about my parents after that—home alone without me.

Then I devoted a couple of minutes to Shoshi Rubinstein. She had asked me to send pictures of camp. Her family was saving money for her sister's college and could not afford a vacation. I told her sure, I would send pictures.

But I had forgotten I wouldn't have a phone!

Was Buck's new no-electronics policy going to ruin Shoshi's summer?

Just before the camp bell rings, there is a faint sound like a warning. I had not remembered this sound till that moment when I heard it again—the distant creak of the wooden tower responding to the first tug on the bell rope.

Then . . . ding-*dong!* Ding-*dong!* Ding-*dong!*

The first full day of camp had begun!

I threw back my sheet and got out of bed. I went into the white tiled bathroom. I washed up. I brushed my teeth. I came back out. I put on Levi's shorts and a plaid short-sleeved blouse, which is like a camp uniform on days you don't go riding. At home it would be a tank top, but in the sun here, sleeves are better.

I folded my pajamas and put them away. I made up my bunk.

I did all this quickly and quietly, keeping out of everyone else's way.

Meanwhile, Hannah had to wake up Lucy three times. And Olivia had curled up in a ball and moaned, "I am never coming back to this horrid, horrid place!"

Emma sat down at the foot of Olivia's bunk and consoled her: "You'll feel better when you've had some orange juice."

On the way to breakfast, I could not help it. I was grinning. It was a normal morning in Flowerpot Cabin. I was really back at camp.

When the bell for start of activities rang at nine a.m., Lucy looked at Hannah. "What now?" she asked.

"We covered this at breakfast!" Hannah said.

"Riding assignments and sign-ups," Emma told her. "We can walk over together, okay? But first you should put on more sunscreen."

At camp, your riding assignment—either morning, afternoon, or evening—is a big deal because which of the other activities you can do depends on it. Like, there is no photography if you get morning riding because photography only happens in the morning, and there is no archery if you ride in the afternoon because archery only happens in the afternoon.

We had all submitted our riding requests from home, and now the assignments were posted on the side of the barn. By the time we got there, other kids were already clustered around the printed sheets, trying to find their names.

Vivek was not one of them.

"I got morning!" Olivia pumped her fist. "Yes!"

"Me too." Emma grinned. "What horse did you get?"

Olivia looked back at the sheet. "Shorty. Huh. Who ever heard of a horse called *Shorty*? My boots will be dragging in the dirt! What riding did you get, Lucy?"

"Afternoon," she said.

"Me too," I said. "And my horse is Katinka."

"Oh, I had her last summer," said Emma.

I remembered something about Emma's horse last summer. "Is she the one that bit you?"

"Only once, and it wasn't her fault," said Emma.

"What do you mean it wasn't her fault? Did she think you were a carrot?" I asked.

Emma laughed. "You just have to watch out when you saddle her."

Emma is too nice, I thought. If you ask me, one bite is one bite too many. But it's tough to switch horses. Maybe Katinka had learned better manners since last summer.

Activity sign-ups took an hour. I picked leatherwork and—it was Lucy's idea—watercolor painting. After that, we had a hydration break, which is how they say "juice boxes" at camp. Then it was time for me and Lucy to go out to North Corral to meet our horses, and for Emma and Olivia to go to the pool for the mandatory swim test.

If you are getting the idea that Moonlight Ranch is almost as organized as school, you are getting the right idea. This is why my parents like it. It is not possible to laze away your summer at Moonlight Ranch.

To get to North Corral, you go to the campfire pit and keep going. Then you turn left up a steep path till you come to a big flat place surrounded by aluminum fencing, and that is it. You are there.

That afternoon, about fifty campers were making the short hike. None of them, if you are wondering, was

Vivek. Apparently, "soon" meant later than right now, late morning on the first full day of camp.

The sun felt powerful on my back, but I knew it was not nearly as powerful as it would be later in the day. The sky was as bare of clouds as the corral was of plants. The horses had gnawed to nothing any green that had ever dared sprout here. All of us—kids and counselors—were wearing hats and carrying water.

Ten counselors met us. In charge of them was Cal. I remembered him from last summer because he was tall and a real grown-up, not a college student like most of the others. Even so, he had chubby cheeks like a baby.

"Hey," he greeted me. "It's Grace, right? Good to see ya back again."

Cal had never been my leader for anything, but I was not surprised that he knew my name. There are some Indian-American kids at camp (Vivek, for example), but I am the only girl who looks like me, and I was the only one last year too. Here at camp, I am used to being memorable.

Meet-Your-Horse works like this. Each counselor

takes five campers and, one by one, finds and halters their horses. I had only ridden a few times before I came to camp last year, but I had learned a lot in one summer. Now I knew how to catch a horse, bridle it, groom it, saddle it, and ride it. I knew the parts of the horse, the parts of the saddle, and the parts of the bridle.

When I put my mind to something, I am usually good at it.

Cal put a halter on Katinka and brought her over. She turned out to be a red paint, which means a white horse dappled with strawberry-brown markings. She was fourteen hands high, Cal told me. One hand equals four inches, and fourteen of them is small for a horse, but that meant we fit. For an almost eleven-year-old, I am small too.

Katinka greeted me by dipping her nose and flicking her ears forward; she was interested but not annoyed. I rubbed the velvet softness around her nostrils, and she snuffled at me, probably hoping for oats or a carrot. I thought of bringing up the biting thing, but Katinka and I had just met, after all. I didn't want to be rude.

CHAPTER EIGHT

Grace

By lunchtime, all of the cabin flags had been hung up on cords suspended between the ceiling beams in the mess hall. The doors opening and closing created drafts that made the flags flutter. Even with so many tarantulas, the room seemed festive.

Flowerpot Cabin's giant chocolate chip cookie was in the center of things—right over the silverware caddies. It looked excellent. Some real country should use the cookie symbol on its flag someday. Who wouldn't be happy to pledge allegiance to a cookie?

The horse-poop flag—*ewww*—had been hung in a far corner.

Olivia and I arrived at lunch at the same time. Hannah wasn't there yet. I had just sat down and was thinking about sandwiches when—at last!—I spotted the back of Vivek's head. It was attached to the rest of him and sitting three tables away with the other boys from Silver Spur Cabin.

Did I feel relieved? Did I feel happy? Did my heart-beat speed up a little?

I cannot say for sure because I did not have a chance to think. Right away, Olivia saw him too and elbowed me. "Grace! *Look*!"

"I know—*shhhh*! Don't stare, O!"

"Go talk to him!" She practically shoved me off the bench.

"That's okay. I don't have to—," I started to say.

"Is that Vivek?" Emma sat down and leaned over me to get the mayonnaise.

"Grace *refuses* to go talk to him," Olivia said.

"That is not true! I just do not want to bother—"

"Here he comes!" Olivia announced.

My stomach clenched, which was not my fault; it was Olivia's. She was making such a big deal out of everything.

I did not look up. I did not want to see him and smile too wide, or worse, act all jittery and embarrassed. Instead, I concentrated on a blue bowl full of peanut butter set out in the middle of the table, and I waited to hear Vivek's voice over the hum of talking and eating noises in the mess hall.

He would say, "Hi, Grace," and I would be casual, "Oh, what a surprise, Vivek. It's you."

But that's not what happened. I didn't hear Vivek's voice at all. Instead, it was Olivia again. "Oh, never mind. He's talking to Lucy."

"Wait . . . what?" My gaze left the bowl of peanut butter fast and found Vivek and Lucy, standing by the milk station and laughing about something. Then Vivek went back to his table, and Lucy came over to ours with her glass of milk.

Vivek never even looked in my direction.

Olivia pounced the second Lucy sat down. "Why didn't you bring him to say hi? *Someone*"—she nodded at me—"is *dying* to see him!"

Lucy seemed surprised. "Vivek? He just got here." She started to make herself a peanut butter sandwich. "I'm starving. Has everybody done Meet-Your-Horse? Mine's called Spot 'cause he's a pinto. It's not a very original—"

"Lucy?" Emma interrupted. "I think Grace has been kind of curious about why Vivek's late getting to camp. Do you know why?"

Lucy said, "Yes."

I said, "Emma, it's okay. I can speak for myself."

"So in that case"—Olivia looked at me intensely—"why don't *you*, Grace, ask *her,* Lucy, to tell *us* why Vivek was late getting to camp. *Okay*?"

Most people think of me as quiet and nice—shy, even.

But most people are wrong.

I have what my father calls a "volatile" temper. It means that when I lose it, I go the tiniest bit ballistic. It does not happen often. Last year at camp, it did not happen at all. . . .

Which explains why my friends were so shocked when I suddenly stood up from the lunch table and said: "WOULD YOU PLEASE LEAVE ME ALONE ABOUT VIVEK? IF I WANT TO TALK TO HIM, I WILL!"

Since no one else in the mess hall happened to be speaking loudly at that moment, everybody in the mess hall heard me. This was unlucky.

Another unlucky thing was how I knocked over my glass when I pushed away from the table, and milk splashed everywhere, and then the glass rolled off the table's edge and fell to the floor and broke—*crash!*—into a million sharp and tiny pieces.

Now everyone at lunch was looking in my direction, even Vivek.

It was five or six minutes later that the full force of *embarrassed* hit me. By then I had stomped through the main doors and out of the mess hall and into central camp, where I was pacing under the cottonwood trees—ten steps right turn, ten steps right turn, ten steps right turn, ten steps right turn—making perfect squares.

Why was I such an idiot? Why was Olivia such an idiot? Why did she have to make such a big deal out of everything?

Because of her I was hungry and alone, and I could never face Vivek, ever—not if we were the last two people on Earth, or at Moonlight Ranch, either.

CHAPTER NINE

Vivek

It was funny how my new bunkmates were impressed that I knew Lucy.

They had all seen the clip of her from the TV, the one where she sounded all extra-humble the way a super-hero always does before she (or he) suits up. Anyway, we were at lunch, and my counselor, Lance, had just introduced me around to my new bunkmates, and I got up to get milk and ran into Lucy, and she asked why I was late getting to camp, and I told her, and then I sat back down again, and the guys were all like, "*Dude!* You *know* her?"

"Uh, yeah," I said, feeling the tiniest bit cool about it. "We're friends."

"It's brave what she did," said Jamil, who is almost as tall as Lance and skinny and from Cleveland. "Plus, she's hot."

Hot? I had never thought about Lucy that way. In my mind, "hot" is a word that goes with singers and models, not people you actually know.

"If you say so," I said, and then Zach changed the subject.

"Sorry you got such a lousy bunk," he said, "but Jamil here—he insisted on the single, and Lance let him have it."

"I'm claustrophobic," Jamil said. "Can't stand being closed in by the ceiling or a bunk above my head."

"Poor, poor baby," said Zach.

I started to say I didn't care what bunk I got, but before the words left my mouth, Grace stood up and yelled at Olivia, then everybody turned to look.

At first I didn't even didn't realize my name was part of it—then Jamil said it was and added, "So I guess that Asian girl's your friend too, right? And I guess she's crazy?"

"I never used to think so," I said.

If that sounds lame, please consider that I was really sleepy at the time. I had taken a night flight from Pennsylvania to D.C., and then a red-eye to Phoenix. That was all my dad could get when he changed my ticket. A van had picked me up early in the morning at the airport and brought me here. When I arrived, there was just time to throw my bags in Silver Spur Cabin and come to lunch.

I had been looking forward to seeing Grace, actually. Now I looked over again, and saw she was going out the door. Was she okay? And where was their counselor, anyway? On the first day of camp, counselors usually eat with their campers. I could see Lance at the salad bar right now—going wild with the bacon bits.

I might've gotten up to ask about her . . . except I had

just constructed for myself a cheese and tomato sandwich that could only be described as epic.

And I was *so-o-o-o* hungry!

My mouth watered as I prepared to take the first bite.

Whatever was up with Grace, the girls would sort it out.

CHAPTER TEN

Olivia

So Grace put on quite the performance in the mess hall, and after it all of us sat still for several seconds, brains blank, mouths open. Since when did quiet, perfect Grace throw tantrums?

Let me just say, it was more than *my* mind could fathom!

At the same time, there was one thing I wanted to

make perfectly clear: "You guys," I said, "what happened just now, you know it wasn't my fault—right?"

Lucy aimed her big unblinking eyes at me. "You shouldn't tease Grace about Vivek," she said.

"I wasn't teasing!" I protested. "I was *encouraging*."

Emma had stood up from the table by this time. Where was she going? "You were bossing her, O," she said. "And no one likes to be bossed."

This was more than I could take. "Seriously, Emma? That is pretty amusing coming from you."

"What's that supposed to mean?" Emma asked.

"Only that you're the biggest boss of all!" I said.

"Hoo boy," said Lucy, under her breath.

I fight with my brother, Troy, all the time, and he fights back. Now I expected Emma to do the same, but she didn't. Instead, she turned toward the kitchen and walked away.

"What the heck!" I looked at Lucy. "Do my armpits smell? Everyone is abandoning me!"

"Only Grace abandoned you," said Lucy. "I'm still

here, and Emma just went to get stuff to clean up the spill. See?"

Lucy was right. Emma was coming back. She had a broom, a dustpan, and a rag. Her face was all pouty. Without looking at either Lucy or me, she started sweeping up broken glass. I wondered where Hannah was, anyway. Cleaning up seemed like a counselor kind of job.

"Look, Emma," I said, because apparently more clarification was needed. "I am sorry to be the one to tell you, but you *are* bossy. It might be that you can't help it, but still it is a fact. Jenny says when you recognize a character flaw in yourself, you should take the opportunity to correct it and become a better person. So maybe that's what you should do, Emma. No offense."

"Jenny is your housekeeper, right?" said Lucy.

"Wow—good memory," I said.

"Sometimes good, sometimes bad," said Lucy. "What do housekeepers do exactly?"

Emma answered before I had the chance. "They clean rich people's houses."

"Hey, you take that back," I said.

"Which part?" Emma asked.

"Which part of rich people's houses do they clean?" Lucy said.

"Not that," I said. "The part about rich people. And also everything else, Emma. Besides, Jenny doesn't clean our house. She cooks and takes care of us."

Emma had swept up the last of the glass. "I am not taking anything back—except for this broom to the kitchen. Then I am going to see about Grace. Remember her? Who wants to come with me?"

CHAPTER ELEVEN

Grace

On a scale of one to ten, my surprise at opening the door of Flowerpot Cabin to find Hannah there crying her eyes out rated ten.

Hannah is our counselor! She is the one with all the answers!

She is calm, beautiful, kind, and smart.

And now she was standing by the one lonely desk in

the room, staring into the wastebasket on the floor, and sobbing!

What could our calm, beautiful, kind, smart counselor who was *twenty years old*—a *grown-up!*—possibly have to cry about on the second day of camp?

We hadn't even done anything bad yet!

Maybe there was something dead in the wastebasket. One time last year there was a mouse running around Flowerpot Cabin. Could it be a dead mouse in the wastebasket? Would a dead mouse be enough to make Hannah sad?

Or what about a tarantula—like the ones on the flags? Except I am not sure that a dead tarantula would be that sad. Speaking for myself, I'd be more likely to scream if I found a dead tarantula.

As these thoughts raced through my head, I stood paralyzed in the doorway. Hannah hadn't even noticed me yet. Maybe I could turn around quickly and get away before she did.

But what if she needed help?

I wished it was Emma who had found Hannah like this. Emma would have known what to do. Emma would have given Hannah a hug, or said just the right thing.

At last, Hannah looked up. "Oh, hi, Grace." She wiped the snot trail under her nose and sniffled. "Oh, sorry."

My face must've looked as surprised as I felt because Hannah laughed at me through her tears. "It's not that bad, honey. I'll live."

"What happened? Are you okay? I mean, not to be nosy or anything. Did something die?"

Hannah sniffed back another sob, then smiled bravely. "You could say that. But if it's all the same to you, I'd rather not talk about it. I'm sorry I missed lunch. Oh, gosh"—she looked at her watch—"and there's an equine orientation in the Black Barn in five minutes. Grace, tell me the truth. Do I look okay?"

No! Hannah did not look okay! Her eyes were red and puffy. There were tear streaks on her cheeks and snot streaks on her lips.

But if I said that, it might make her feel worse!

"Uh . . . ," I stalled. "Okay for what purpose?"

Hannah smiled another brave smile, squinched her eyes to wring out the last tear, and tugged on her hair. "Okay. I get the message. And I guess I can be a couple of minutes late."

Two doors lead out of the bunkroom of Flowerpot Cabin. One goes outside to the flagstone walkway and the other to the white tiled bathroom. Hannah ducked into the bathroom and, a second later, I heard the water gushing from the tap.

I stood rooted to the floor of the cabin, my thoughts in a whirl, till finally she emerged. "Better?" she asked me.

"Better." I nodded.

"All right, then, Grace, my friend," she said—and you almost would've thought she'd never been crying at all. "I'll be back right around the end of siesta, got that? Make sure the Flowerpot girls are on their best behavior before then. You're supposed to get some rest—remember?"

CHAPTER TWELVE

Grace

It wasn't long after Hannah left that Emma, Lucy, and Olivia surged into Flowerpot Cabin. They must have run from the mess hall in a pack.

By this time, I had forgotten I was mad at Olivia, and I wasn't thinking of Vivek.

I was thinking of one thing only: Hannah crying!

Bursting to tell someone, I blabbed the whole story

the instant my bunkmates came through the door.

"Wait, Hannah was *crying*?" Olivia said.

"Yes!" I said.

"Like tears-coming-out-of-her-eyes, crying?" Emma said.

"I believe that is the definition of crying," I said.

"Counselors aren't allowed to cry, are they?" said Lucy.

"Whether they are or not, Hannah was," I said. "When I came in here, she was looking down at the wastebasket, crying."

"Hannah. Our counselor. Hannah," said Emma. "Crying."

"Why was she looking at the wastebasket?" Lucy asked. "Why was she crying?"

You can't blame me for getting annoyed, right? Any sane person would have!

I decided to tell it one more time. I spoke slowly. I enunciated. "I came into Flowerpot Cabin. I heard sobbing sounds. I looked up. There was Hannah—"

"Wait," said Emma. "Was she crying?"

And that's when Olivia started to laugh. She has a great laugh, heartfelt, musical, and most of all, infectious. Emma caught the bug after that, and soon they were laughing so hard that they couldn't stop. I'm not sure I could have told you why, but I started laughing too, and finally so did Lucy.

Laughing felt good—even if it did make my sides ache. I realized then that none of us liked being mad at each other.

Eventually, I recovered enough to say, "We shouldn't be laughing. Hannah was *so* sad. . . ."

"So sad she was crying," said Olivia.

"Who was crying?" said Emma.

"*Hannah* was crying," said Olivia.

"Tears"—I giggled—"coming out"—I laughed—"of her eyes . . . *crying*." I had to gasp the last word, and soon we were helpless again, until finally Lucy managed to ask, "But *why* are we laughing? It's mean to laugh!"

"No, it's not," said Emma, who is never mean. "We're not laughing *at* Hannah."

"We're laughing," I tried to explain, "because I had to

repeat *three times* what happened when I walked in to get Oreos."

"Oreos?" Emma perked up.

"What Oreos?" Lucy asked.

Oh, shoot. I never meant to mention my Oreos. There is a secret stash hidden in a pocket of my suitcase. We're not supposed to have food in our cabins in case it attracts pests, but Oreos don't count as food exactly. Oreos are more like emergency rations.

"I missed lunch." I shrugged. "I was hungry."

Olivia said, "This whole thing is totally my fault. I never, ever should have teased you about Vivek. I am really, really sorry."

Wait—was Olivia actually apologizing? This added an extra dose of surprise to my already-mixed-up emotions. Trying to unscramble them, I breathed in and out. "It's okay. My dad says I have a volatile temper."

"'Volatile' is a good word," said Lucy. "So the reason we're laughing is that you had to repeat yourself. I get it. Ha-ha-ha."

"It's not just that I had to repeat myself," I said.

"It's that I had to repeat myself three times."

Emma looked at Lucy and explained, "It's the three times that makes it funny."

"I said 'ha-ha-ha,'" said Lucy. "Didn't I?"

"I see Lucy's point," Olivia said. "Put that way, it doesn't sound funny."

"I guess you had to be there," said Emma.

"I was there," said Lucy.

"We know!" said Olivia, Emma, and I, and after that, we couldn't help it, we busted up laughing again . . . Lucy, too.

Here is something I learned that day. After a while, a person is all laughed out. When this finally happened, Emma made an announcement. "It is now one thirty-seven. Siesta is over at two fifteen."

"We have to hurry," Olivia said.

"Hurry with what?" asked Lucy.

"Isn't it *so totally obvious*?" said Olivia. "It is up to us, the members of the Secret Cookie Club, to fix Hannah's life!"

"Step one," said Emma. "Find out what's in the wastebasket."

CHAPTER THIRTEEN

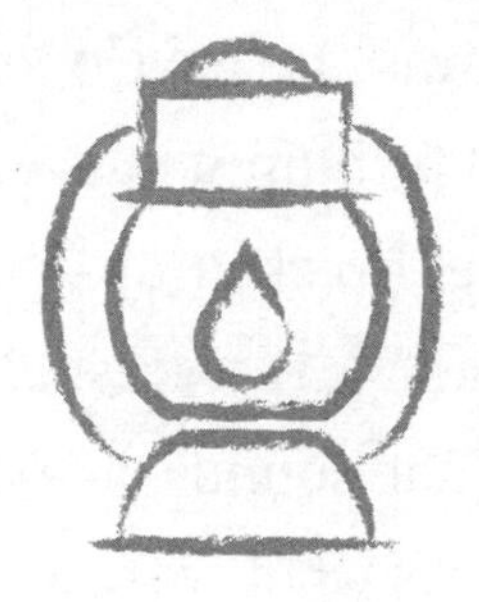

Grace

Before I could stop her, Olivia picked up the wastebasket and flipped it over.

"Did you *have* to do that?" I asked.

"Do you want to help Hannah or not?" she said.

"Anyway, it's done," said Emma, nudging the pile of trash with her toe. "So let's see what we've got."

The wastebasket had been less than half full. Nothing in it was gross. Most of the contents were pieces of colored construction paper from when we made the flags. Other than that, there was an envelope, some camp-store receipts, and some torn-up scraps of printer paper with typing on one side. I picked up a printer-paper scrap and read it out loud: "'. . . greatest girls I ever . . .'"

Emma said, "That sounds like a letter, a letter to Hannah, and I bet it's what we're looking for. She tore it up because it was bad news, and then she started to cry."

"Wow," said Lucy. "How do you know that?"

"I read a lot of Nancy Drew," said Emma.

Olivia's eyes were shining. "This is all really, really *dramatic*!"

I said, "Let's get to work."

Emma separated the pieces from the rest of the trash. I studied the shapes and the words on each piece, then handed it to Lucy. She glued the pieces onto a leftover sheet of construction paper we had found on top of the desk.

Meanwhile, Olivia, who is not the most patient person in the world, lay down on her bunk.

Treating the assembly job like a jigsaw puzzle, I

handed Lucy the pieces that had straight sides first, because those must be edges. Then I started looking at the words to see if I could arrange them in sentences and paragraphs.

"I think Emma is right—it's a letter," I said shortly, "because here's the salutation—'Dear Hannah'—and here's the date, 'June twenty-third.'"

"Sometimes I forget to put dates on letters," said Lucy, studying a scrap to see if it was the right shape to fit beneath the one that read "June."

"I always put the date on," I said.

Emma said, "Aha! A clue! The writer is someone more like Grace than like Lucy."

I didn't like the sound of that. "Are you saying I'm the kind of person who would make Hannah cry?"

Emma shrugged. "Are you?"

"No!" I said. But in the meantime I'd had another thought, an attack of conscience. "Should we even be doing this? It *is* Hannah's personal correspondence."

"And Hannah is our *personal* counselor," said Olivia from over on her bunk.

"She needs us," Emma agreed.

"Besides, I am *dying* to know what the letter says!" said Olivia. "Hurry it up over there, can you? Who's it from? Can you tell yet?"

"You *could* come and help us," Emma said.

"I *am* helping. I'm the lookout," said Olivia. "If I see anybody out the window, I'll sound the alarm. What do you think—'ding-ding-ding-ding-ding'? Or 'squaw-aw-aw-awk'? Or maybe a siren, like—"

"Olivia!" I said. "You're giving me a headache!"

"Oh, yeah? Well, you're giving me a *complex,*" said Olivia.

"No signature yet," said Emma, ignoring us.

"What about the envelope?" I asked.

"Here it is—and it's in one piece." Emma pulled it out for inspection. "No return address, but the postmark is New York, New York."

Olivia sat up, raised her arms, and began to sing: "'A heckuva town! The Bronx is up and the Battery's down! The people ride in a hole in the ground—New York, New York, it's a—!'"

"Olivia!" Emma and I interrupted. Even Lucy had stopped working.

"What was that even about?" I asked.

"It's from the musical *On the Town*!" said Olivia. "Duh—don't you guys know *anything*?"

"I know *The Lion King* and *Beauty and the Beast*," Emma said.

"I know *Wicked*," I said.

"Wicked?" Olivia's face lit up, she opened her mouth, and some telepathy told me she was going to sing "Popular." No way could this be allowed to happen. "*Olivia,*" I said, "*we are trying to work over here!*"

"Oh, *fine.*" Olivia lay back down on her bunk.

The edges of the paper were in place by this time. Piecing together the middle was trickier. You had to look at both the logic of the words and the outlines of the shapes.

"It's from someone named Travis," Emma said.

"He signed it 'Love always,'" I added.

"Which is pretty funny," said Emma, "because look at this."

All along we had been working fast in case Hannah came back. Now that we saw how personal the letter was, we worked even faster. We knew our counselor wouldn't like us snooping. But it was for her own good.

"Here." I handed Lucy the beginning of a paragraph, then I asked Olivia if she saw any sign of Hannah outside. Olivia didn't answer, and I tried again: "O-*liv*-i-*ah!*"

Again no answer.

Emma got up on her knees and swiveled to see Olivia's face. "Wake up!" She tugged one of Olivia's toes, causing Olivia jump. "*What?* Is she coming?"

"How would we know? *You're* supposed to be watching," said Emma.

"Well, sor-*ree*!" Olivia rubbed her eyes. "I can't help it if we have to get up before *dawn* around here. I wasn't cut out for guard duty."

"Done," Lucy announced.

Emma leaned over her to look. "OMG! You can hardly tell this paper ever used to be torn. You did a great job, Lucy."

"I know," said Lucy.

Olivia rolled her eyes. "Enough with the lovefest over there. What does the letter say?"

I returned the wastebasket to its spot. Lucy laid the paper on the desk. Emma studied it a moment and then read out loud:

Dear Hannah,

I hope your flight to Nevada was smooth and that you arrived okay at Camp Moonrise. How are your girls? I hope they are getting along.

Hannah, I have something difficult to write, and there is no point in procrastinating further. I want to break up with you. I hope that wasn't too mean of a way to say it, but we said we would always be honest. Didn't we?

You are a great girl, one of the greatest girls I ever met. It has been really cool being your boyfriend. Any other boyfriend you find will be really lucky to have you as a girlfriend. If he doesn't realize this, or if he doesn't treat you good, then you can have him call me, and I will set him straight.

LOL. I hope you don't mind my little joke. Just trying to cheer you up a little.

Maybe by now you have already met a good-looking guy counselor who is less of a jerk than me. If so, that would be great because then I wouldn't feel so terrible about breaking up with you.

Except maybe I would feel jealous, and how crazy is that? LOL.

From this you can see I still care very much.

The reason I am breaking up with you is I met another girl who is also great. I didn't mean to meet her. It just happened. Her name is Jennica, if you care. It is okay if you don't.

Have a good summer with your girls. I hope it is not too hot there, but I bet it is. It's the desert, right? LOL.

Love always, your friend,

Travis Spooner

P.S. Say hi to your parents for me.

Nevada?

Hello-o-o!? The camp was in *Arizona*!

Not to mention he got the camp's name wrong!

Not to mention, who signs a breakup letter "Love always, your friend"?

And then there were all those stupid "LOLs" like he was some kind of second grader!

Emma shook her head. "It's Jennica I feel sorry for."

"Me too," said Olivia. "Hannah is lucky to be done with this loser."

"How could a counselor have been so dumb?" I asked.

"Love *is* dumb," said Lucy.

"Don't say that!" said Olivia. "And anyway, Travis Spooner does have one good idea."

Emma looked up at her. "What's that?"

Olivia's lips had formed a tiny secret smile. "That part about a good-looking counselor?" she said.

"Hmmm," I said, and I realized I was smiling too.

But before we could even share what we were thinking, there were footfalls outside, the door creaked, and Hannah's voice behind us said, "What is it you girls are looking at, anyway? You're supposed to be resting!"

"Nothing!" all four of us said at the same time.

Meanwhile, my heart went bump. We were busted for sure! The letter was right there on the desk, and Hannah would see it the second she looked down.

Only . . . she didn't. Because when I looked back at the desk, the letter had disappeared, and the only evidence of what we'd been doing was the yogurty smell of wet glue lingering in the air.

CHAPTER FOURTEEN

Lucy

The instant I heard Hannah outside, I whisked the letter from the desk into the wastebasket.

Now the only worry was if Hannah happened to glance inside it and see the letter in one piece again. Would she believe the explanation was miraculous intervention from God?

Probably not.

"Well, whatever you girls were doing," Hannah said,

"siesta is over, and it's time to get a move on. Emma and Olivia, you're coming with me to North Corral, right? Meet-Your-Horse?"

Emma and Olivia nodded and went for their hats and water. At the same time, their eyes kept darting to the wastebasket, like they feared the letter might leap out and give us away.

Grace, meanwhile, was making a lot of noise opening and closing the drawers of her bureau. "Lucy and I have the swim test," she said. "Uh . . . but I . . . uh, I can't find my bathing suit."

"Oh, dear," said Hannah. "Are you sure you packed it?"

"It's here somewhere." Grace shoved a drawer shut. "It's just going to take me a couple more minutes. You guys should get going, though, Hannah. It's a long way to North Corral. Lucy will wait for me—won't you, Lucy?"

"Sure," I said.

Truthfully, I was kind of liking it that Grace couldn't find her bathing suit. Usually she is the most organized person on the planet. Was it possible that for once she had messed up and lost something?

No. It wasn't.

The moment Hannah, Emma, and Olivia walked out the door, Grace hurried to the wastebasket and pulled out Travis's letter, then tore it into a thousand pieces.

"Now if Hannah looks, at least it won't be obvious," Grace said. "Tomorrow during chores, we can empty the trash."

"Good thinking," I said. "So I guess you knew where your suit was all along?"

"Of course." Grace displayed the rolled-up beach towel she'd pulled from her top drawer. "It's in here with my goggles. Let's go."

The Moonlight Ranch swimming pool is on the other side of Boys Camp. Since obviously a girl can't go through Boys Camp, we had to skirt the fence and then walk past the camp office.

We talked about Hannah and Travis and what four campers could possibly do to help her feel better. Then, just where the Boys Camp fence turned one way and we turned the other, Grace said, "So, Lucy, I have a question." She was trying hard to sound casual, and she was failing.

"Ask it," I said.

"Why was Vivek late getting here? You said he told you, right?"

"He did tell me," I said, "but it's private."

Grace spun around, eyes flashing. *"What do you mean it's private?"*

I stopped walking. "Grace, are you going to go ballistic again? Because if you are, I want to be ready."

Grace snapped, "I will if I want," but once the words were spoken, her anger was gone, and she kicked a toe in the dust. "Look, Lucy. Here's the thing. There's this person deep inside me I don't like very much. I call her Snot-Nosed Grace. Sometimes she comes out, and it's like I can't help it."

"Snot-Nosed Grace," I repeated. "That's funny. I guess maybe there's snot-nosed versions of most people."

"Do you think so?" Grace asked. "Is there a Snot-Nosed Lucy?"

I had been happy when I'd thought Grace had lost

her swimsuit, hadn't I? "Yes," I said. "There is."

"So I guess I'd better watch out," Grace said. "But, uh . . . can you tell me *why* it's private?"

"Snot-Nosed Lucy?" I said.

"The reason Vivek was late!" Grace said.

"Oh, that," I said, but what to say after that? Telling her why would be telling her what—and then it wouldn't be private.

"You were laughing when he told you," Grace prompted.

"How do you know that?" I asked.

"Because I was watching," Grace said.

"That's creepy," I said.

"It's not like I have a crush on him," Grace said.

"Okay," I said—even though her denying it convinced me that she did. My mom's been on a romance roller coaster pretty much my whole life. One thing I've learned is that human feelings often operate backward.

Grace was still talking, but my own thoughts distracted me. The swimming pool was going to feel so nice. Maybe there'd be pasta with pesto for dinner. What should I paint tomorrow in watercolor activity? Maybe a picture of my horse, Spot.

"'Spot' is a dumb name, don't you think?" I asked.

"Wait, what?" said Grace. "Lucy, were you even listening?"

"Ye-e-es," I said, wondering (but only a little) what she had been saying. "But don't you think—"

"Lucy, look!" Grace stopped in her tracks and so did I. We were almost to the pool by this time, and here came Vivek walking toward us on the path. He was wearing blue swim trunks. His hair was dripping wet. There was a red towel around his neck.

He said, "Hi, Lucy. Hi, Grace."

I said, "Hi, Vivek."

Grace didn't say anything. When I looked over, I saw she looked the way a fly probably looks when it's just been paralyzed by a spider. I mean, if you could see the fly's face, which I never have, but we learned about how spiders paralyze their prey in science. It's cool, so long as you don't happen to be the fly.

"Look, Grace!" I finally said. "It's Vivek! That's a shocker, huh?"

It was a stupid thing to say, but the alternative was standing there till the end of time. And besides, it worked. Grace said, "Hi, Vivek" in an almost normal voice. Then she said, "It's very nice to see you. That is, I already saw you. We were in the mess hall at lunch. But it's very nice to see you, uh, here on the path to the pool. How are you doing?"

At this point I wouldn't have blamed Vivek for wondering about Grace's mental health. First she yelled at Olivia in the mess hall, and now she was talking crazy. But if this was on his mind, he didn't say so. Instead he explained that since he had gotten to camp late, he'd had to take the swim test during siesta, and now he was going to his cabin to change before going to North Corral.

"So, Vivek," I said, "how about if you explain to Grace why you only got here today."

"He doesn't have to," Grace said, "not if it's private."

"Private from who?" Vivek said.

"Private from me," Grace said.

"Why would it be private from you?" Vivek asked.

"I have no way of knowing," Grace said, "because it's private from me."

"Lucy?" Vivek looked at me. "Are you confused too?"

"No," I said, because I wasn't, and also because this conversation was boring and I was ready to go swimming. "Can we go now?" I asked Grace.

"My mom is having a baby," Vivek said.

"She is?" Grace's jaw dropped, and then she grinned. "But that is *so exciting*!"

I grinned too. "Can't you totally picture Vivek as the best-ever big brother?"

"I can," Grace said, "but I'm still confused. Is that is why you got here late?"

"Yeah, kind of," Vivek said. "My parents were supposed to go to India this summer. The baby's not due till October. But then my mom had some pains, and the doctor said she shouldn't go so far away."

"So you stayed home an extra day to make sure your mom's all right?" Grace said.

Vivek nodded. "And it looks like she is, and the baby, too, but she has to get a lot of rest."

"Can I ask one more question?" Grace said. "Why did you tell Lucy not to tell me that?"

Vivek looked at me. "I didn't."

I said, "He didn't. It's just a private kind of thing. A thing it was Vivek's business to blab, not mine."

Grace shook her head. "I'm not sure I understand you, Lu."

I sighed. "That's okay. No one else does either."

CHAPTER FIFTEEN

Lucy

Just as she promised, Paula distributed the mail at lunch each day. At first no one got much, and I didn't get anything. But by the end of the first week of camp, all of us in Flowerpot Cabin had received letters.

Mine was a fat brown envelope that came on Friday. I looked it over while sitting on my bunk after lunch. Emma was there, but the siesta bell hadn't rung yet, and no one else was back.

"Who's it from?" Emma asked.

"The triplets I babysit and their mom, Kendall," I explained. "Here. You can see if you want."

Dear Lucy,

Your camp can't possibly be eight weeks long, can it? Did you know there are 1,344 hours in eight weeks? I used the calculator on my phone.

I have hired another girl to come over to wrangle the triplets starting tomorrow. Meanwhile, to preserve the collective sanity, Arlo, Mia, and Levi are watching a lot of SpongeBob.

Anyway, cross your fingers about this other girl. As you know, my darlings can be a handful.

They have drawn some pictures for you, which are enclosed.

Have fun at camp!

Love,

Kendall

P.S. Seventy-two hours down. Only 1,272 to go.

"Wow—I think she really misses you," Emma said.

I giggled. "I know. And look at the pictures the kids sent."

The first one showed what looked like an openmouthed brown animal with big teeth. It was standing on its hind legs and leaning over a tiny human stick figure with a yellow blob on his head. The blob might've been hair. A speech bubble like the ones in cartoons said, "Hep!!!!"

"Is that supposed to be Arlo?" Emma asked.

I nodded. "That's the way he draws. And I think the letters are supposed to say, 'help.'"

"Oh, I get it," Emma said. "He wants you to save him from another wolf."

I studied the picture again. "Or possibly a bear?"

"Either way, he definitely sees you as fierce," Emma said.

I handed her the next picture. It reminded me of Olivia's flag—only don't ever tell her I said that, okay? The drawing took up the whole page—a giant face with red lips, blue eyes, black lashes, and pink dots for nostrils. From the eyes to the bottom of the page there were lines of little circles in every color.

"Tears?" Emma guessed.

"Mia can be kind of a drama queen," I said.

The last one was from Levi. Instead of drawing his message, he had written it in red crayon: "Com bak rit now!"

Emma laughed. "Do you miss them, too?"

"Kind of," I said. "But when I'm busy here, I don't think of them that much."

"Are you going to write back?"

"Sure," I said. "But I bet this is the last letter I get from them. When the new babysitter comes, they'll forget all about me."

Only I turned out to be wrong.

The Fourth of July was the next week, and on the day after that I got another fat envelope. There was no letter from Kendall this time, but there were two drawings that I think were supposed to be fireworks, along with another note from Levi. This one said: "Plis com back rit now!"

I wondered if the added "plis" showed the new babysitter's influence. Maybe she was teaching them good manners.

Before dinner that night, I wrote a reply.

Dear Arlo, Mia, and Levi,

Thank you for the beautiful drawings. I have tacked them up above my bunk bed so I can admire them every day. Levi, I am afraid I can't come back yet because camp isn't over. I am glad you miss me, though, because I miss you, too.

Yesterday was Fourth of July. Buck,

the camp director, does not believe in fireworks because (he says) they spook the cattle. So instead of fireworks we had a barbecue outside. But guess what? Nature decided there were going to be fireworks whether Buck wanted them or not, and she provided a huge storm.

It was really pretty looking across the desert into the sunset and seeing chains of lightning as tall as the sky. The loud cracks scared some kids but not me. In the end, the rain part lasted only a few minutes, but we still had to move the picnic inside.

Boo-hoo.

How do you like the new babysitter? I am sure she is really nice and makes good snacks and plays good games. Even so, please don't forget me.

Tell your mom and dad hello. Remember too much SpongeBob turns tender brains to mush.

Love,

Lucy

CHAPTER SIXTEEN

Olivia

Camp sessions are eight weeks long. Every two weeks, you change out activities—like from archery to silk screening, or pottery to jazz dance—but even so the days start to blur together. Our letters home were due every Sunday. If you missed a Sunday, you got demerits, so none of us in Flowerpot Cabin would ever have dared to miss.

What if you were the person who kept us from winning Top Cabin?

How bad would that make you feel?

The first Sunday, I had written to my parents, so on the second one I decided to write to Jenny and Ralph. They have lived with our family and helped us out since before I was even born. Jenny cooks and supervises the housecleaners, the gardeners, and the pool guy (and sometimes my mom and dad, too); Ralph works in the yard and repairs whatever needs repairing.

I told Jenny once that this division of labor of theirs was sexist. (We were doing a social studies unit on sexism at the time.) And Jenny told me she and Ralph were only doing what they were best at. She said biscuits baked by Ralph would poison us, and if she fixed the AC, it would blow up.

"I know there are men who cook and women who maintain machinery," Jenny explained. "But those men and women don't happen to be Ralph and me."

The next day I raised my hand and explained this to my teacher, Mr. Driscoll, and he said Jenny had made an excellent point. Then he said, "Thank you for your input, Olivia. And now you may sit down."

I wrote my letter to Jenny and Ralph while lying on my bunk during siesta. I propped the paper against a book on my knees. I used a purple gel pen. I was surprised how hard it was to form letters one by one instead of typing them on a keyboard. It seemed like I could hardly remember how! But I wrote slowly and carefully, and in the end, this is the letter I wrote:

Dear Jenny and Ralph,

Camp is super fun!!!

It is super hot here!!!

I am super fine!!! (LOL)

My horse's name is Shorty. He is not so super. He is lazy. He is white and—guess what—SHORT!! In watercolor activity on Friday, I painted a picture of Shorty. It doesn't look that much like him because how is a person supposed to paint white on a white piece of watercolor paper???

I made him brown instead. I told him this

the next afternoon while I currycombed him, and he said it was okay, he forgave me. At least I think that is what he said. Sometimes it is hard to understand four-legged language. LOL.

Probably you are wondering about the other members of the Secret Cookie Club (shhhh!) so I will tell you. Grace's birthday was last week. Do you remember that last year we made cookies to celebrate?

That is not what we did this year. This year her parents sent a cake all the way from Massachusetts! It was packed in dry ice and puffy silver foil. It was pink with roses and a little smooshed, but you know what? That didn't hurt the taste one bit! In the mess hall, everybody sang, and Grace blushed, which was so, so, so cute!

Besides normal camp activities, the Cookie Club membership has its own special project to mend our counselor's life, which was almost annihilated by her evil and clueless boyfriend—EX-boyfriend—Travis.

How we are going to mend her life is to **ENGINEER A ROMANCE** between her and the hunkiest counselor at Moonlight Ranch, Lance. I am sticking on some heart stickers sent by Mom to show you how dreamy he is:

So far we have not found time to make a detailed plan because we are **SO BUSY** simply being at camp and participating in so many healthy activities!

But we will find time!

And when I see you at the end of summer, I will tell you how it all turned out.

Don't worry. We won't do anything very bad. Also, don't tell my parents.

Lots and lots and lots and lots and lots of love,

Your very, very, very favorite, one and only
OLIVIA

P.S. How are you? Is it super hot there? Are my parents fine? If you run into them, please tell them hello from their only daughter.

CHAPTER SEVENTEEN

Olivia

Can I be brutally honest here?

No one could possibly adore or admire the other members of the Secret Cookie Club any more than I do . . . but without *my* verve, *my* energy, and *my* compelling personality, our counselor Hannah's life might have remained *forever in the toilet!*

As it was, the membership came up with a complex and comprehensive Plan to Fix Hannah's Life, which we then named PFHL, which is pronounced "piffle."

In my estimation, carrying out PFHL should have taken no more than two weeks max. The way it turned out, though, it actually required most of the summer!

The first challenge was finding a hole in our crazy-supervised camp schedule when we could talk over our ideas and agree on what Mr. Driscoll would call our "implementation timeline." It didn't help that Hannah, sad and mopey over the loss of that rat Travis, spent way too much time frowning in Flowerpot Cabin and way too much time sticking like glue to the four of us. Little did she know her dedication to her campers was working against her happiness!

I thought of trying to explain this to her, but in the end I rejected the idea. Officially, the membership didn't know a person called Travis had ever existed. She had never told us about him, and she never found out we had reconstructed his letter. Also, it was possible she wouldn't like the idea of four eleven-year-olds running her love life. As our housekeeper, Jenny, likes to say, people don't always know what's good for them.

It wasn't till the third Thursday of camp that an announcement signaled we were about to get the time for planning. We were at lunch, and Buck rose from his table to say he was calling a counselors' meeting for that night. No emergency, just paperwork issues. The meeting time was nine forty-five, fifteen minutes after lights-out.

That day I was eating with Haley from Purple Sage and McKenzie, from Manzanita, a twelve-to-thirteen cabin. We are all in the same swim group. As soon as Buck finished speaking, I looked everywhere in the mess hall and one by one found Emma, Grace, and Lucy—each one at a different table, each one smiling, each one with the same thought as me: *Tonight!*

"All right, girls. I'm going," Hannah said on her way out the door. "Don't stay up too late whispering, okay? I hope I'm back soon."

"Good night, Hannah!" we chorused.

When the door clicked shut, I counted to ten. "I hope it's not too soon," I said.

"But just in case, we should talk fast," Grace said. "Who is in charge of this meeting, anyway? You, Emma?"

"Not me," Emma said.

"I don't mind doing it," I said.

"Doing what?" Lucy said.

"PFHL!" Grace said.

Lucy giggled. "Piffle to you too!"

And after that, we got down to work.

CHAPTER EIGHTEEN

Emma

If a teacher assigned you to write a list of adjectives to describe me, Emma Rosen, not a single one would be "sneaky." This failure of mine is not a problem most of the time, but it is a problem when you're carrying out a plan like PFHL.

In fact, if you want the whole truth, my trouble with PFHL isn't only lack of sneaky.

My trouble is that I'm not graceful and athletic like

Grace, or brave and quick-thinking like Lucy, or beautiful and outgoing like Olivia.

I am just normal. Normal smart. Normal looking. Normal nice.

My only special quality is this: I am good at organizing. At home when my friends do a project, they put me in charge because they know the project will get done, and they won't have to worry about it.

Here at camp, the Secret Cookie Club membership had been ready to put me in charge of PFHL, too—then I said no. Remember that time when Olivia called me bossy at lunch? It hurt my feelings. And I decided then and there I wouldn't be the boss of anything at camp this summer.

Let someone else worry for once.

So Olivia took over PFHL planning the night Hannah was at the counselors' meeting, and actually, Olivia did okay. We made a plan. We got assignments. We even came up with a timeline. We were feeling pretty proud of ourselves—not to mention sleepy—when Lucy said, "What if Lance has a girlfriend already?"

Olivia yawned. "Then they'll just have to break up."

"But that's not fair," Lucy said. "What if his girlfriend is nice?"

"No one is as nice as Hannah," Grace said.

"Besides, who has time to worry about random unknown girls?" said Olivia.

I said, "Uhhh . . ."

And Olivia said, "Uhhh . . . what, Emma? And hey, are you okay over there? We haven't heard from you in a while. Are you worrying about your assignment?"

Olivia couldn't see me, if you're wondering, because this planning session took place in whispers with all of us on our own bunks in the dark.

We had to be super quiet. Everyone at camp knows Buck has sentries patrolling the walkways after lights-out. No one has ever seen or heard these sentries. They always wear black camo, and their sneakers have special silent soles. Still, we campers know they are there. Their main job is keeping girls out of Boys Camp and vice versa, but they also listen for disturbances.

If you make a disturbance you get demerits, and there go your chances to make Top Cabin.

A ten-to-eleven cabin that won Chore Score *and* made Top Cabin? Flowerpot would be a legend!

"I'm fine. I'm awake. I'm listening," I whispered. "And if Lance has a girlfriend already, I don't think we should try to fix him and Hannah up. It's encouraging him to cheat, and it's not nice."

"That's what I think too," said Lucy.

Olivia must have sat up fast because her bunk bed squeaked. *"So we did all that PFHL planning for nothing?"*

"Shhh!" Grace and I hissed.

Olivia grunted, lay down, and whispered, "So we did all that PFHL planning for nothing?"

"No," I said. "Or maybe. Or yes—but only if Lance has a girlfriend."

"So in that case, *you* find out, Emma," Olivia said. "You're the one that's so interested in fairness to a girl none of us ever even heard of."

"Okay," I said, "I will."

"And you have to do it fast," said Grace. "Because till you do, we can't start on PFHL at all."

"Okay," I said again. And then, as my friends fell asleep, I lay there wondering how.

CHAPTER NINETEEN

Emma

Olivia's not the only one who hates the wake-up bell at Moonlight Ranch. I do too. But last summer I learned that I can make myself get out of bed if I focus laserlike on one thing: pancakes.

The ones at Moonlight Ranch are extra delicious, and you can get them every day, not just on weekends. To go with your pancakes, there's cinnamon sugar, maple syrup, applesauce, sunflower seeds, and mini chips. You can have all you want, but if you have all at once, your tummy will suffer.

I know this from personal experience.

Every morning as I got ready for the day ahead, I played a pancake countdown in my head: Wash face, brush teeth, fold up jammies:

Pancakes.

Straighten sheets, pull on jeans, button blouse:

Pancakes.

Out the door, down the walk, to the mess hall:

Pancakes!

That day in the mess hall, I sat down at the table with my pancake-stacked plate, had a drink of milk, cut the first bite, and bit into it—*ahhhh.*

Pancakes made getting out of bed worthwhile.

Now that I was fortified, I decided to ask for advice in finding out whether Lance had a girlfriend. The one helpful thing I'd thought of was this: Jamil—one of Lance's campers—has morning riding with me. Maybe he knew. But how would I get him to tell me?

"Start with small talk," said Grace, who is much sneakier than me.

"Define small talk," I said.

"You know, like 'How are you,' 'I'm fine,' 'What's new,' 'Not much,' 'Does Lance have a girlfriend . . . ?' Like that." She shrugged.

"OMG, you call *that* advice?" said Olivia, whose plate had eggs, strawberries, and a double portion of potatoes on it. "I have a much, much, *much* better idea! Bring up a related subject that seems totally innocent but isn't."

"Oka-a-ay . . . so like what?" I asked.

"Lemme think," Olivia said. "Maybe you just happen to mention something about *your* boyfriend or your *ex*-boyfriend. And then you go on to talk about boyfriend-girlfriend as a general kind of a category, and after that, Jamil says something, and you say something, and Jamil says something . . . and soon the state of Lance's romantic life has been revealed."

"Yeah, but O," I said, "I don't *have* a boyfriend, and I never did."

"Make one up," said Grace, whose breakfast was a bowl of rainbow-colored sugar cereal.

"I don't think I'm that creative," I said.

"Not a problem," said Olivia. "You can borrow mine."

"What?" I said.

Olivia laughed. "I don't mean borrow a real live human boy. I mean pretend a boyfriend I used to have is yours. That way you don't have to invent him from nothing. Now, what do you want to know?"

Lucy looked up from her granola. "Did you say you have a boyfriend, O?"

Olivia shrugged. "Lots of 'em. But nobody special now. The one I'm thinking of is from the beginning of the school year."

"Was he white, black, Latino, or other?" Lucy asked.

I was pretty surprised by that question, and I guess Olivia was too. "Why is that important?" she asked.

"It's just one of the questions," Lucy said. "If you'd rather, you can tell me his religion, political party, last book read, and approximate household income."

"Approximate . . . *what*?" Olivia looked at me, then at Grace. "What is she talking about?"

"No idea," said Grace.

Lucy giggled. "It's what they ask on dating websites. I look at them sometimes with my mom."

"O-h-h-h," said Olivia. "Now I get it. In that case, he was a black kid at my school, one of the few. And he was *an older man*—in the seventh grade! And I don't know about his political party, but his last book read was probably *Hatchet*—"

"That's a good one," said Grace.

"—and I don't know about religion either, but I don't think he's Jewish because he gave me a Christmas present. Since we broke up, his name is unimportant, but if you want to know, it was Brian."

"Why did you break up?" Grace asked.

Olivia made a tragic face, looked at her eggs, and sighed. "Physical incompatibility."

Grace said, *"Seriously?"* while I both wanted and did *not* want details.

Seeing our expressions, Olivia laughed and shook her head. "*You guys!* All I mean is he was shorter than me! We looked terrible together in pictures."

At Moonlight Ranch, chores are after breakfast, and that day mine was the most despised of all: shower, toilet, and sink.

In my belly the pancakes contended with orange juice as I squeegeed the shower walls and scrubbed the floor. As I worked, I tried to picture myself saying, "Good morning, Jamil. I have a black boyfriend named Brian who's probably Christian and in seventh grade. How are you?"

Meanwhile, Grace was sweeping the bunkroom, and Lucy was dusting. Olivia's job was to sweep the walk outside. When I was done, she would come in and clean the mirror.

Later, after we left for activities, a counselor would come around to inspect the cabin and score five categories: bathroom, surfaces, windows, beds, and overall tidiness. Some counselors barely inspect at all; others give you zeros for a single dried-up bug wing on the floor.

When the bell rang for activities at nine o'clock, Grace did a preinspection. This had been Hannah's idea to keep us competitive.

Grace took preinspection way seriously. She strode through like the sergeant in a war movie, hands behind her back, turning her head right and left. She even peered under the beds and behind the toilet. Anytime she found anything bad, she pointed at it, then at the person who had failed to meet her high standards.

Poor Grace. She was trying to be firm, but she was more like comical, and that morning Olivia followed behind, mimicking her every move. Lucy and I tried not to laugh, but Olivia was hilarious, and finally we busted up.

Grace was not amused. "Do you girls want to win or *not*?"

"Lighten up a little, shee-*eesh!*" Olivia said. "We *will* win. We're the best. That Brianna girl doesn't have a chance."

"We won't win unless we're serious," said Grace. "And whatever you think about Brianna, O, *she* got Purple Sage Cabin a Dandy Dust Mop, and we don't have anything like that."

"Oh, yeah? Well, no mop can beat our elbow grease!" Olivia said.

"Ewww," said Lucy, checking out her elbows.

"Let me guess," I said. "Is that something Jenny says?"

"Bingo!" Olivia pointed. "It means 'hard work.'"

I said, "We gotta go, you guys. Got your hat, Lucy? Is everyone wearing enough sunscreen? You too, O. Even dark-skinned people need sunscreen."

"I *know,* Emma," said Olivia.

"Just checking," I said.

Finally we were ready to file out the door, Grace and Olivia to first activity, me and Lucy to riding. Since campers all leave at the same time, it was morning rush hour on the walkways and paths of Moonlight Ranch.

CHAPTER TWENTY

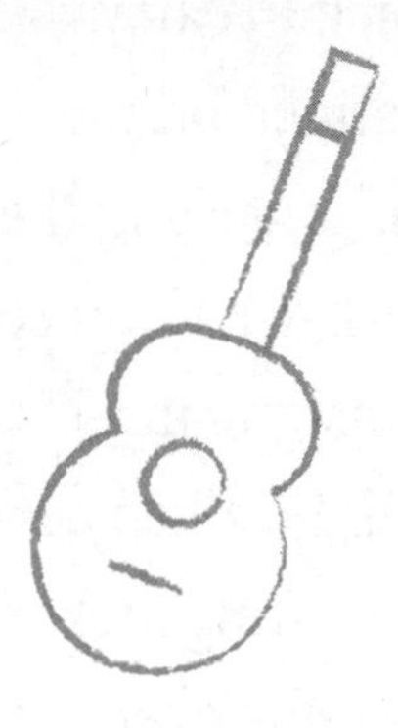

Emma

Lucy and I picked up our bridles in the horse barn as always, then walked the short distance to North Corral to catch our horses. Mine was a palomino mare called Sunshine, seventeen hands high with a star on her forehead and a sock on her right foreleg. To me, she was beautiful. I even liked the warm-hay-and-dust smell of her.

There is something comforting about a horse. It's big. It's solid. It's reliable. It counts on you for food and grooming. You count on it to carry you around. Even that time last year when Katinka bit me, I didn't blame her. I had been saddling her, squeezing the cinch around her middle. How would you like it if someone did that to you?

That day I found Sunshine in a cluster of horses near the center of the corral. I walked carefully around their swishing tails to avoid getting kicked, then came up on her left and tossed the reins over her neck.

"Good morning," I said. "Sleep well?" Sunshine nuzzled me and blinked her big eyes. "Okay, open up now." I clicked the bit against her front teeth till she parted them and clamped down. After that I pulled the bridle over her ears and buckled the straps. "Ready? Let's go get a saddle on, whaddaya say?"

I gave a gentle tug to lead her out of the corral. Meanwhile, all around me campers were doing the same thing—bridling their horses and taking them out the gate and down the hill to be saddled. Among them was Jamil. His horse was a bay called Zippety, which lived up to its name, always walking fast near the head of the line on trail rides.

I took one breath for courage, then launched into small talk. "So, Jamil, how are things in Silver Spur Cabin?"

If I had said, "So, Jamil, aren't those zombies I see by the fence?" he could not have looked more surprised. In fact, he turned his head to see if I was talking to someone else. Then he must've remembered he's the only Jamil at camp. "How do you know I live in Silver Spur Cabin?"

I knew for about two hundred reasons. Because we were both ten-to-elevens. Because we had been at camp three weeks. Because I don't keep my head buried in a feed trough the way the average clueless boy does.

Most of all I knew because Lance was his counselor, and I was trying to fix Lance up with Hannah.

None of those answers fit in with my small-talk strategy, though.

"I guess I know because Vivek's my friend, and he's in your cabin too," I said.

Jamil said, "Oh," but I thought he sounded suspicious.

By this time we had joined the parade of campers and

horses walking down the path to the horse barn. Since we were walking together, we ended up tying our horses side by side. Then we went in and got currycombs and brushes.

You have to groom the horse before you saddle it. That's what they teach you at Moonlight Ranch.

"Vivek is friends with a lot of girls," Jamil said as we worked.

Woot! That was small talk, right? All of a sudden, this was going *much* better than expected. Too bad I couldn't think of a better reply than, "Uh-huh."

"He's friends with that Lucy girl too," Jamil went on. "Do you know her?"

"Yeah. We're in the same cabin. She's right over there." I nodded toward Lucy, who had come down the hill ahead of us and was already saddling Spot.

"Yeah, I saw her." Jamil stood on tiptoe so he could look over his horse at Lucy. "She's really, uh"—he paused—"brave."

"You mean about the coyote," I said. "I know."

After that I was out of things to say and still no

closer to Lance's love life. Was I going to have to take desperate measures? Mention my fictitious older boyfriend? Maybe. But first we had to return the combs and brushes and lug out blankets and saddles.

Western-style saddles are heavier than the English kind, and last year I had a hard time hefting mine over the horse's back. This year it's easier. I know I'm taller, and maybe I'm stronger, too.

Since this was Jamil's first year at camp, Cricket, a seven-eight-nine counselor, came over to help him thread the latigo through the cinch rings and then make sure the cinch was tight enough. If it wasn't, the saddle would slide off.

I have to admit it made me feel a little bit superior that I didn't need any help.

How you mount a horse wearing a Western saddle is you stand on the horse's left side facing its tail, put your left foot in the stirrup (otherwise, you end up standing in the air backward, and I'd rather not say if I know that from personal experience), and step up into it while swinging your right leg over the horse's back.

One thing you never ever do is grab the saddle horn. That marks you as a tenderfoot for sure. Instead, you hold the reins and the horse's mane in your left hand and the cantle of the saddle with your right.

When we were all astride our horses and circling them around by the barn, a kid named Theo asked, "Where are we going anyway?"

Three counselors were leading us that day, Cricket, Matt, and Gail. Cricket answered, "Cider Creek Wash. How does that sound?"

"Sure!" "Where again?" "Do we get to canter?" asked various campers.

"These horses have a full day ahead of them," Matt said. "We'll have to see."

Morning riding lasts from nine fifteen to noon, but the actual on-your-horse part is about ninety minutes. The counselors pick a destination four miles away and a route that loops around. Sometimes we have time to stop and go for a canter in a safe flat place where the horses won't trip. Other times we're just sightseeing.

I have noticed that some horses trudge like hauling a person is a pain, but Sunshine isn't that way. She likes having a kid aboard. She lifts her hooves neatly, arches her neck, raises her head, and moves her ears alertly to hear the sounds of birds, the breeze, horses' hooves, and human conversation.

By this time, I had recovered from the sore thigh muscles that go with riding a horse when you haven't in a while. I tried to ride the way I'd been taught: sit up straight, square my shoulders, flatten my tummy, allow my lower body to move in sync with the horse's gait.

Leaving camp, I admired the rugged and rocky landscape, so different from what I'm used to at home. The scenery where I live in Pennsylvania is dominated by gray sky, green trees, and black asphalt. Here in the high Sonoran Desert, the rocky earth was pink and gold, the sky a brilliant blue, the grasses and cacti sage green. Because the air was so clear—very little moisture and no pollution—the colors seemed to glow. Looking around, I couldn't help but feel happy, which made me feel confident, too.

Surely I could find out whether Lance had a girlfriend.

I touched my heels to Sunshine's flanks so she'd catch up with Zippety. "Hey, Jamil," I said, suddenly inspired. "So, uh . . . in Silver Spur Cabin . . . do you guys have any, like, decorations on the walls?"

"Such as party decorations?" Jamil said.

"More like pictures, I was thinking. You know, photos of your family or maybe your special friends from home?"

"I have a picture of my new nephew on my phone, but—of course—no phone," said Jamil. "I still can't even believe that. I'm always patting my pocket."

I said, "Oh, I know," to be friendly, but really I was used to being without it by this time. "So, no photos for decoration, huh? What about Lance?" I forged ahead. "Does he have photos of *his* special friends, like, uh . . . maybe on his bureau or anyplace?"

Jamil turned his head to look at me. "That's a weird question."

I bristled. "No, it's not. It's small talk."

"Whatever," said Jamil, "but why do you care about Lance's pictures?"

"I don't!" I said, and then I had nothing else to say, so what did I do? I kept talking. "Our counselor, Hannah, has photos," I said, which was a lie, but Olivia had encouraged me to be creative, right? "I just wondered if having photos was a normal thing for counselors."

"No idea," said Jamil. "Hey, aren't you in the same cabin as that other crazy girl, Grace?"

"Grace isn't crazy," I said, but then I remembered her yelling at Olivia in front of everyone at lunch.

"Says *you*," Jamil said, and I could tell he thought I was crazy too, like it's some kind of Flowerpot Cabin thing.

I decided to try a more usual question. "So, where are you from?"

"Why?" Jamil said.

"I'm from near Philadelphia," I said.

"And that Lucy girl is from California, right?"

I looked around. "You can talk to her yourself, if you want. She's right over there."

"No, no, that's okay," he said hastily. "I wouldn't want to bug her or—"

"Hey! *Lucy!*" I called.

"Oh, jeez. Now you're *yelling*," he said.

Lucy rode up on my left. "Jamil wants to talk to you," I said.

"Hey, Jamil," Lucy said.

"Hey," Jamil said.

"What do you want to talk about?" Lucy said.

Jamil was very tall for a kid our age, but now he slumped down like he wanted to be as small as possible. "Just, like, uh . . . where you're from and all," he said. "I mean, I heard about you and the coyote. I guess you're really brave."

"Thank you," Lucy said. "I guess you're really brave too."

"I am?" Jamil said.

"Probably," said Lucy.

From what I could see, Jamil and Lucy were going to get along great—or better than Jamil and me anyway. Since my first try at small talk hadn't gone so well, I pulled back on Sunshine's reins to slow her down. This way, Jamil and Lucy could ride side by side while I tried to think up new questions.

As we rode on, the counselors pointed out landmarks, and Matt explained the differences between a butte, a mesa, and a plateau. Meanwhile, I fell in next to Kate, whose horse was a black named Lightning. I had heard she was homesick, so I asked if she was feeling better. I told her I was homesick last year at first too.

"I am feeling better," she said. "Thanks for understanding. I think some people thought I was being a baby."

"The weird thing is, when you get home, you'll probably miss camp," I told her. "That's what happened to me."

"Can I ask you something?" Kate said. "How come you guys call yourselves 'the membership'?"

"Where did you hear that?" I asked, surprised.

"Brianna told us. No offense, but she thinks that proves you're all stuck-up."

"We're not!" I said.

"Oka-a-ay," Kate said. "So what does it mean, then?"

"I guess I see how it sounds bad," I admitted. "But it's more like a joke we have than anything. Do I seem stuck-up?"

"No," she admitted. "Not right this second anyway."

"Want some sunscreen?" I asked, and one-handed, took the tube out of my fanny pack, then reached across and handed it to her. "I think your nose might be getting burned."

Kate took the tube, applied a white blob to her nose, and handed it back. We were almost to Cider Creek Wash by then. There, we reined in our horses, dismounted, stretched, and ate apples and granola bars from the counselors' saddlebags.

"Now drink some water!" Gail commanded.

As always, somebody had to complain that the water in our canteens was warm, and somebody else had to make a joke about ice cubes and refrigerators in the desert.

"Drink up or shrivel up," Cricket said. "Take your pick."

Along with everyone else, I took a good long drink.

Then—to be on the safe side—I reapplied sunscreen too.

Lucy and Jamil stuck together on the way back to camp, so I talked to Kate some more and also to another girl, Mallory, who lived in Stirrup Dot Cabin.

Back at the barn, we returned our saddles and saddle blankets, rubbed down the horses, led them back up to the corral, and removed their bridles.

I patted Sunshine's rump, and she snorted.

"See you tomorrow!" I said. Then I looked around for Jamil. This was it, my last chance to find out what I wanted to know. When I saw him, he was still talking to Lucy. Why was she hogging him? Had she forgotten I had a job to do? That would be just like her.

On the path down to the barn. I caught up with them and cleared my throat. Lucy looked over and smiled. "Oh, hi, Emma. Are you getting a cold?"

"I'm fine," I said. "Uh . . . so . . . Jamil . . ."

"Now what do you want to know?" Jamil asked.

The way he said it made me want to apologize for breathing air and occupying space on the planet, but I couldn't afford to be snarky. "I have this seventh-grade boyfriend and he's not Jewish and—"

Lucy started to laugh.

"*What?*" I scowled at her.

"Nothing." She squelched her smile. "I'm sure that boy is nice. Doesn't he sound nice, Jamil?"

"Uh . . . right," said Jamil.

What the heck? Did clueless Lucy even know she'd foiled my last chance to find out Lance's romantic status?

Worst of all, I'd have to tell Olivia and Grace that I'd failed.

I was fuming when I hung up Sunshine's bridle, and the second I got Lucy alone, I was going to tell her so, too.

Only that didn't happen.

I caught up with her on the way back to central camp, but before I could say a word, she did: "Lance doesn't have a girlfriend, Emma. He told his campers he used to, but they broke up right before he came to Arizona. So the coast is clear for Hannah."

Here's something weird about anger. It stays around

even after its cause has gone away. So now I was left sputtering. "How did you find that out? You're not even sneaky!"

"I know I'm not, so I just asked him." She sounded hurt. "I thought that you'd be happy."

"I am," I snapped.

"You don't sound like it," she said.

"I know." I exhaled a long breath, and some of my anger went with it. "I'm sorry," I said. "But didn't he think it was weird when you asked him?"

Lucy shrugged. "He did, but he said it was less weird than when you asked about party decorations in Silver Spur Cabin. What was that about?"

CHAPTER TWENTY-ONE

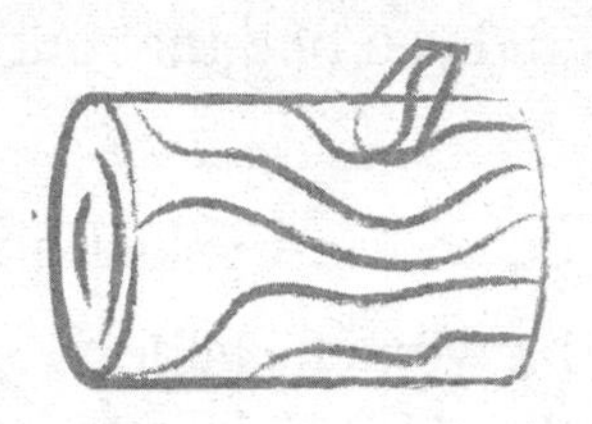

Vivek

Two strange things happened the third Friday I was at Moonlight Ranch.

First, my bunkmate Jamil came over to our table at lunch and sat down with his plate of food, and started talking all "hot Lucy this" and "hot Lucy that," and he would not shut up.

Luckily, I had constructed a generous and filling turkey sandwich with provolone on a kaiser roll. It was delicious; it kept me busy and diverted. Without it, I don't think I could have put up with Jamil's nonsense.

At last, Jamil said, "So she likes me, right? That means she likes me?"

I chewed and swallowed and sipped my ice-cold milk before answering. "I don't know very much about girls."

"Why else would she bring up Lance's girlfriend?" Jamil asked.

"Maybe she likes Lance," I said.

"That's ridiculous," Jamil said. "He's a counselor. I think she was trying to be sneaky by bringing up girlfriends. She was hoping I'd volunteer information about myself. See?"

"No," I said.

"Oh-h-h, so *now* I understand," Jamil said. "You're jealous!"

"No," I said again.

"Look, Vivek, don't feel bad," said Jamil. "Some of us got it, and some of us don't."

The kid sitting across from us was Luke, another of

my bunkmates. He is from Phoenix—and even so he hates the heat at Moonlight Ranch. Phoenix is hotter than here, so you'd think he'd be used to it, right? But not at all, and go figure. Now Luke started to laugh. "Got *what,* exactly, Jamil? Germs? Fleas? Cooties?"

I laughed too, and Jamil scowled. "You don't have to be insulting," he said.

"That wasn't insulting," Luke said. "Trust me, if I want to insult you, there'll be *no* question. Anyway, dude, seriously, I hope you and Lucy are very happy together."

This shut Jamil up, and I got to enjoy the last bites of my turkey and provolone in peace. I made a mental note: Thank Luke.

It was after lunch that the second strange thing happened. It also involved the girls from Flowerpot Cabin.

Something was up with them. It's like they were *haunting* me.

Always before, I had liked Grace Xi because she is serious and good at things. I even gave her a present on the last day of camp last summer, a very small one. That yelling incident in the mess hall was strange, but since then she had seemed as normal as any girl. I had been thinking sometime I'd go over and say hi during free time before dinner, but there was always some distraction.

Anyway, forget that. Now I know that she is crazy too. Never mind Lucy. Grace and Jamil ought to team up.

After lunch ends, there are fifteen minutes till siesta. That equals thirteen minutes to hang out with your friends and two minutes to sprint for your cabin so you don't get demerits. I was sitting on the top rail of the fence in central camp with Luke when Grace came up and said, "Hi, Vivek. Can I talk to you?"

I said, "You are already are," and smiled. At this point I did not yet realize she's crazy.

"Just us, I mean," she said, and blushed, which was when I became suspicious.

Luke hopped down from the fence. "I guess I know when I'm not wanted."

"Hey!" I tried to call him back, but he waved without turning around.

Now Grace was really blushing.

"What is it?" I said.

"If I asked, would you do me a favor?" she said.

"Are you going to ask? Or is that just hypothetical?" I said.

"I'm going to ask," she said. "And it's not just for me. It's for all of us in Flowerpot."

"Okay," I said. "Ask."

Grace swallowed and looked at her feet. Finally, she said, "One day soon, someone will give you a plate of cookies and a sealed envelope. We want you to put them on top of your counselor's pillow."

Whoa! Did I just walk into a spy movie or something?

In fact, the request was so weird I might have laughed out loud except that Grace looked super-serious. So I said something entirely reasonable: "Why?"

"It doesn't matter why," Grace said. "It's just a favor."

"I can't do it if I don't know why," I said.

"Why can't you?" Grace said. "Don't you trust us?"

"Trust is not the problem," I said. "I might be happy to do it. But it's bad policy to agree to do things you don't understand."

When she had blushed, Grace's cheeks had turned

pink. Now they glowed positively red. *"I can't tell you!"* she said.

"So *I won't do it*!" I said.

I had mimicked her tone of voice, hoping she'd laugh, but this was a bad miscalculation. She stomped her foot—actually stomped her foot!—glared at me, and said, "Stupid *boys*!"

Then she turned and marched toward Girls Camp.

"Sorry," I said to her retreating back. But I wasn't really sorry. I was thinking that girls sure can be unreasonable.

CHAPTER TWENTY-TWO

Olivia

Boys sure can be unreasonable.

Even a mostly nice one like Vivek.

It was the start of siesta, and we four members of the Secret Cookie Club were on our bunks. Grace had just told us Vivek's reaction to our request. Hannah could walk in anytime.

"I've got bad news too," Emma said. "I checked with Mrs. Arthur, the cook, and she said she can't give campers permission to use the kitchen, only counselors."

"That problem at least is easy peasy," I said. "We will ask a counselor to help us."

"But what counselor?" Emma asked.

"I have an idea, and I'll let you know at dinner," I said. "The real problem is who's going to put the cookies on his pillow, and I'm afraid there's only one solution."

"What?" Grace asked.

"We do it ourselves," I said.

"But girls aren't allowed in Boys Camp!" said Grace.

"Are you forgetting the sentries?" said Emma.

"They'll never catch us," I said. "We will move like the wind."

"And by 'we,' you mean *who* exactly?" Emma asked.

"I mean all of us—*duh.* We are in this together."

My bunk was on top and Emma's was beneath me. I rolled onto my belly and hung my head over the edge of the mattress to look at her. Just as I suspected, she was rolling her head side to side on her pillow, shaking it *no*.

Ever since we started PFHL, I had been waiting for Emma's natural-born bossiness to come roaring back.

Now—at last—it had.

"With all due respect, O," she said, "it doesn't make sense for us to trek through Boys Camp in a big galumphing herd, carrying a plate of cookies."

"Galumphing?" Grace said.

"So we'll tiptoe," I said, "tiptoe really, really, really *fast*."

Across the room on her own bunk, Lucy giggled.

And Grace said, "I don't like that plan, O. Emma, what's yours?"

"You go," Emma said.

"Wait, *what*?" said Grace. "By 'you,' do you mean *me*? Tell me you don't."

"I can't tell you that because I do," said Emma.

"Wait, what?" said Lucy.

"And she's not the only one who's confused," said Grace.

"Look," said Emma, "of all of us, Grace is the most coordinated, not to mention the most agile, and the strongest."

Grace said, "Uh . . . thank you? I think?"

"Plus you're the smallest," Emma said. "You can get in and out of that window no problem."

"You want me to break in through the *window*?" Grace said.

"Well, how else?" Olivia asked. "It's not like they'll be leaving the door open and the welcome mat out."

Grace was on the bunk above Lucy. Now she rolled over and propped herself up on an elbow to see my face. "O, don't tell me you like this plan too?"

"Emma is making a lot of sense," I said.

"Thank you," said Emma.

Grace rolled onto her back and spoke to the ceiling. "Emma *would* be making a lot of sense except for one crucial fact. I am a coward. *Not* courageous. *Not* brave. In other words, freaked out at the very idea of crossing the border to Boys Camp."

"That does pretty much define 'coward,'" said Emma.

"Don't be silly. You're not a coward," I told Grace. "You told me off in front of everyone in the mess hall at lunch."

Grace shook her head. "That was bad temper, not courage."

"I know—maybe you could harness the power of your bad temper to make you brave," Emma said.

"You want me to get mad at a plate of cookies?" Grace asked.

"Get mad at Vivek," said Emma. "He's the one who didn't do a favor for us; he's the reason you're running a terrible risk."

"Grace could never get mad at Vivek," said Olivia. "Right, Grace?"

"Oh yes, I could," said Grace. "I don't even think I like him anymore. And I *don't* want to be sent home."

"You don't have to do it at all, Grace," said Lucy quietly.

"Yes, she does too!" I insisted.

"Romance is overrated," Lucy said. "Hannah is better off without Travis *or* Lance."

I sat up straight and eyeballed Lucy, who looked totally innocent lying there on her bunk. "Can the rest of you *believe* what you are hearing?" I said. "Where would we even *be* without romance?"

I meant this to be a rhetorical question, which is the kind that doesn't need answering, but Grace started to answer anyway, something about how the word "romance" used to be from Rome.

I ignored this, swung my legs off the bunk, dropped to the floor, and began to pace. In case you can't tell, I was channeling every lawyer that was ever on TV.

"Without romance," I began, "there would no Prince Charming and no fairy tales. There would be no plots to Disney movies. On Halloween, little girls would be forced to dress up as ghosts and vampires and the Mario Brothers because—*hello-o-o?*—what would be the point of *princesses*?"

I paused for breath, then raised my eyes to heaven . . . or anyway, the white plaster ceiling.

"Without romance"—I pivoted to pace the other way—"what kind of a world would it be? I will tell you what kind of a world. A world without proms! A world without Valentine's parties! A world in which candlestick makers and florists and clerks in chocolate shops are *broke* and *homeless* and living on the *street*!

"And what about the poets?" I raised my hands overhead. "*Think* of the poor, *poor* poets! In a world without romance, they would have nothing to write about except the trees and the weather. And who would read those poems? Not me!" I pointed at myself. "And not you either!" I pointed at Emma, who dutifully shook her head.

"Without romance," I continued, "there would be no weddings, people! And you know what *that* means: No flower girls!"

I paused again, just like Mrs. Wanderling taught us in After-School Acting Studio, to gather myself for the big conclusion: "Where would the human race be without romance? I will tell you where! The human race would be . . . *extinct*!"

For a moment, there was appropriately awestruck silence. Then Emma applauded, and Grace murmured, "Wow."

Only Lucy seemed unimpressed. She began to giggle.

I put my hands on my hips and called her out. "How can you laugh? I deserve at least an Oscar for that!"

Lucy stifled her laughter. "You do deserve an Oscar," she said. "But 'extinct' made me think of dinosaurs, and then I pictured them with valentines and red bouquets of flowers."

"Maybe dinosaurs are actually extinct because they lacked romance," said Emma. "Maybe it wasn't a meteor at all."

Lucy said, "Wait—it was a meteor that killed the dinosaurs?"

"Yes, Lucy," Grace said patiently. "And how did you *not* know that?"

"I guess I missed that day," Lucy said.

"We all did," I said, "because it happened sixty-five million years ago."

Emma started to explain. "Lucy doesn't mean *that* day—" But the explanation was cut short by the door opening.

"Hannah!" We all welcomed her.

"Hello, girls." Hannah smiled, closed the door, and threw her keys on the desk. "This looks like a pretty active siesta you've got going on."

"Not really," I said. Then I closed my eyes, reached in front of me, and spoke in a robot monotone. "I am sound asleep and nap-walking."

"Ri-i-i-ight," said Hannah. "So nap-walk right back to your bunk, please, Olivia. I haven't been sleeping well lately, and I'm looking forward to closing my eyes for a few minutes."

CHAPTER TWENTY-THREE

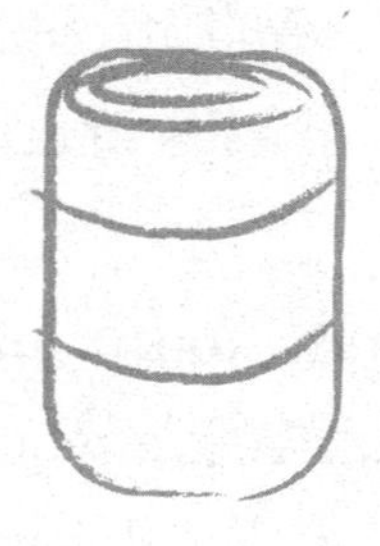

Olivia

Afternoon riding starts right after siesta. That day, Grace and I walked to the horse barn together. On the way, I tried to convince her that she was, too, brave and totally capable of carrying out her new and improved PFHL assignment.

"Think of it as learning a skill," I said. "Like a back-flip or how to multiply fractions. In the end, you will be really, really, really proud of yourself!"

"Is breaking and entering a skill?" Grace asked.

"Absolutely," I said. "And it could be you'll have so much fun you'll take up a life of crime. I hear the money's good."

Grace rolled her eyes. "You're not funny, Olivia."

"Yeah, I am," I said. "Ask anybody. Ask Jenny. Only don't ask my brother. He doesn't think I'm funny either."

We retrieved our horses' bridles from their hooks in the barn and started walking up the hill toward North Corral. We were almost to the gate when Grace said, "There's something I don't get. Why can't we just ask one of the other guys in Silver Spur Cabin to put the cookies on Lance's pillow?"

"Because we don't know them," I said. "They would blab all over camp, and PFHL would be toast. Plus Hannah might be mad."

"How do we know Vivek won't blab all over camp?" Grace asked.

"Because he's Vivek," I said. *"Duh."*

"Okay," said Grace, "if you say so."

"Great!" I said. "So you'll do it?"

"I didn't say that," Grace said. "I just guess you're right about Vivek not blabbing."

"And also you guess you'll do it?" I repeated.

"I'll think about it," Grace said.

You might remember that my horse that summer was named Shorty, and guess what? He *was* short—only fourteen hands high—and dusty white in color, with dirty speckles of gray and brown. Personality-wise, he possessed all the charm of Eeyore, the gloomy donkey friend of Winnie-the-Pooh. Also like Eeyore, his usual posture was head hanging, as if lifting it up required too much effort.

The first time I saw Shorty, I was disappointed. As far as I could tell, everybody else had prettier, happier horses.

But then I decided that Shorty was part of God's plan for Olivia Baron. Just as I was his burden to bear (get it?), he was mine—and I was going to live up to the challenge! I was going to improve that horse's attitude if it was the last thing I did! I was going to boost his morale and raise his self-esteem!

So, along with a bridle and a saddle, Shorty always got a pep talk. "You're a handsome horse and a strong horse, too," I told him. "And you're not even that short, I mean, compared to a pony. Compared to a pony, you are an equine giant!"

If this did anything for Shorty's attitude, morale, or self-esteem, he didn't show it. His head went on drooping as low as ever. And slow? As we moseyed down the trail, crawling ants on the ground overtook us.

Among the counselors in charge of afternoon riding was Jack, the one from Yucca Cabin and the man I especially wanted to talk to. Unfortunately, his horse was a long-legged chestnut, and no pep talk on earth could goad Shorty into catching up with a long-legged chestnut. It wasn't till we all dismounted for snacks and water at our destination for the day, Red Ridge, that I had the chance to tell him that the girls of Flowerpot Cabin really, really, *really* needed a favor.

Now, maybe I should back up a little. For example,

are you wondering why I had picked out Jack as the counselor most likely to assist?

Mostly it was a matter of my well-known *intuition.* Sometimes you just know something, you know?

But if I had to cite a reason, here it is: Because Jack was different. Just from the way he dressed (that old-man hat!) and the way he laughed and the stupid jokes he made, a person could see he didn't mind standing out or bending rules.

I mean, horse poop? Hell*o-o-o-o*? Tarantulas we had in abundance, but no other cabin put horse poop on their flag.

So I explained to Jack that we needed to make a double batch of cookies in the camp kitchen, and I was terribly, *terribly* sorry that I couldn't tell him just *exactly* why, but it was for a good cause, a noble cause, a cause any right-thinking person would wholeheartedly approve.

Hannah's afternoon off was Sunday. Was Jack available? Would he help us?

"Also, it's a total secret," I concluded. "So you can't tell *anyone*."

All this time, Jack had listened attentively to my plea. He hadn't asked a single question. His face had registered no hint of surprise. Maybe people were always asking him for secret favors.

At last I was out of words and waiting for him to reply. It seemed to take forever, but probably it was closer to five seconds. Then he nodded. "Mystery and intrigue," he mused. "I like it! And did you also say there would be cookies?"

CHAPTER TWENTY-FOUR

Emma

When we first started whispering about PFHL, we expected it to take a week or two, and after that we would all high-five and admire the good we'd done in the universe. Then we would get on with our lives.

But it didn't end up being that way. Each step took longer than expected; new steps had to be added. What should we write on the cards that would go with the cookies? How was Grace going to wake up without a phone to put on vibrate? What kind of cookies did Lance like?

He might be one of those people who hates chocolate.

He might be allergic to nuts.

It would have been bad if, after so much trouble, Lance had refused to eat the cookies, not to mention embarrassing (and sad) if they had killed him by mistake.

So Lucy asked Jamil, who had been following her around like a puppy, and Jamil reported back that oatmeal cookies were Lance's favorite—but this piece of spy work took two days because Jamil first asked what was Lance's favorite kind of cake (carrot) and then what was Lance's favorite kind of candy (red jelly beans).

"Jamil must not be the brightest bulb in the chandelier," I said when Lucy reported this. It was after siesta on the fourth Saturday of camp, and the four of us were sitting on the side of the pool with our legs in the water, which came from a spring and felt wonderful. To protect us from the sun, we were wearing hats on our heads and T-shirts over our bathing suits. Even with my legs in the water, I could feel lines of sweat along my backbone.

"When can we go in, Annie?" Olivia wanted to know.

Annie was the CIC (counselor in charge) of the pool that day.

"Hang on. We're still short a lifeguard," she said. "It's times like this I really wish we all had phones."

"It's times like *always* when I wish I had mine," Olivia said.

"I don't think Jamil is dumb exactly," Lucy said. "He claims that talking to me confuses him."

Grace said, "That's fair."

Lucy looked at Grace. "Is it? Why?"

I was afraid of how Grace might answer—sometimes she is not totally sensitive—so I helped her out. "Because you're gorgeous-gorgeous-gorgeous, Lucy! That's how my great-grandmother would say it. You drive all the boys wild."

"You drive Jamil wild at least," said Olivia.

"That's gross," said Lucy.

"Watch out, or Olivia will make another speech," I said.

"Too hot for speeches," Olivia said.

"I'm not sure gorgeous is the problem," Grace said. "Sometimes talking to Lucy confuses me, too."

Shoot—I was afraid she might say something like that. I leaned forward and looked over in case Lucy's feelings were hurt, but from what I could see, she wasn't listening. Her eyes were on a water bug doing laps in the pool.

I was looking at the water bug too, when all of a sudden there was a commotion behind me. It sounded like someone was neighing. . . . *Neighing?*

I turned my head and, yup, that was what it was exactly: *Jack* neighing. Also whinnying, snorting, and braying as he galloped up the path toward the pool, left hand in the air as if it held reins, right hand slapping his own butt.

"Whoa there, Silver!" He burst through the gate, reached the edge of the pool, lurched forward as if he might fall in, then leaned back, teetering, to save himself. "Did somebody 'round here call a *lifeguard*?"

Most of us campers were laughing, but Annie didn't crack a smile. "You're late," she said. "You've kept all these campers waiting."

"Hi-i-i-i, kids!" Jack waved in an expansive arc. "You're not mad, are you?" He put his hands over his heart. "*Please* tell me you're not."

"We're not! We are! We're hot!" came the answers.

"Where were you?" Annie asked.

"Little lady, I would love to tell you," Jack said, "but if I did, I'd have to kill you."

Annie scowled and pointed at the lifeguard stand.

Jack looked stricken. "No, not that!" He got down on his knees. "I'll do anything, anything you say, Annie, but please! Not that!"

Annie ignored him. "Okay, guys, get in the water. But don't any of you go and drown on this guy's shift. He might be too busy cracking jokes to save you."

"Hey," said Jack, getting awkwardly to his feet, "I resemble that remark."

Again, Annie pointed to the lifeguard stand. "Go!"

By this time, even though PFHL was nowhere near full implementation, Hannah was getting better. She no longer had circles under her eyes. Sometimes she even laughed with us. Still, she wasn't the same old Hannah from last year. Like, when she announced, "Lights-out!" or "Hurry up and get to breakfast!" and we argued—because sometimes it is the job of campers to argue with counselors, just as it's the job of kids to argue with parents—she would give in with a sigh that meant, "Whatever. Why do I think I know any better than a ten-to-eleven-year-old anyway?"

Also, a lot of times when we came in from an activity, she was there already, lying on her bunk.

"You should get out and socialize more," I told her one day when I was the first one back from lunch.

"That's what Jane says too," she said.

"Are you okay?" I asked. "Do you think you got sunburned?"

"Nah," she said. "It's just been kind of a tough summer."

"I know." I nodded solemnly. "It's because you've got a cabinful of problem campers."

She smiled. "Hardly. Right now Flowerpot and Purple

Sage have the only perfect Chore Scores in all of Girls Camp."

I already knew we were tied with Purple Sage. But then I thought of something. "*Girls'* Camp?" I repeated. "Not the *whole* camp?"

"Silver Spur has a perfect Chore Score too," Hannah said. "They announced the totals at the counselors meeting last night. Lance was totally trash-talking me too. You girls better beat those boys. If you don't, I will never hear the end of it."

CHAPTER TWENTY-FIVE

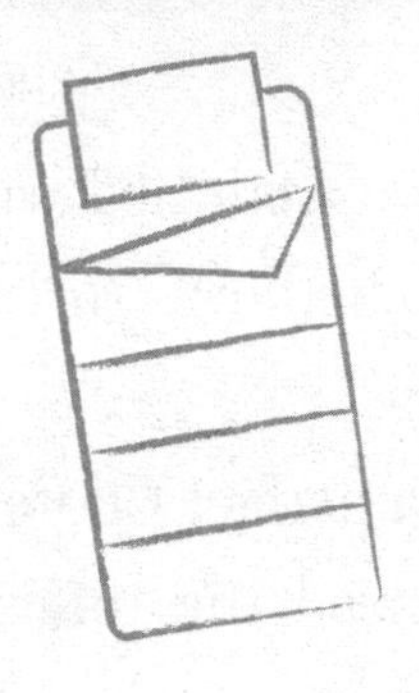

Vivek

On Sunday afternoon, Grace, Emma, Olivia, and Lucy came into the camp kitchen followed by that counselor from Yucca Cabin, Jack.

I know this because I was in the camp kitchen already. I was preparing to make a batch of cookies. I had expected to have the kitchen to myself, so I was surprised to see them—and I guess they were surprised to see me, too.

"*Vivek!*" Olivia was the first one through the door, and you would've thought I was a ghost. "How did you even get in?"

"I unlocked the door," I said. "Then I opened it, and then I stepped across the threshold. Would you like me to demonstrate?"

Grace rolled her eyes. "She means who gave you a key, *obviously*."

"It wasn't obvious to me," I said, "and Mrs. Arthur did."

"Seriously?" Grace frowned. "She wouldn't give *us* one! We had to ask a counselor to come with us and be responsible."

Jack waggled his thumbs at himself. "That's me, the responsible party . . . although, come to think of it, what fun would *that* be?"

I had a feeling Jack had made a joke, but I didn't get it.

"Do you believe Mrs. Arthur gave Vivek a key and not us?" Olivia asked. "How sexist is that?"

"Not to mention it's unfair," said Emma, "since everybody knows girls are more responsible than boys in the first place."

"Speaking of *sexist* . . . ," said Jack.

Olivia took a step back, lowered her chin, and looked at Jack. I knew that look. My mother gives it to me all the time. "Are you saying *guys* are more responsible?" she asked.

"No offense, Jack, but you're a guy and you were late to lifeguard duty yesterday," Emma said.

"Oh, swell," Jack said. "Now the eleven-year-olds are keeping tabs."

"I think I made my point," Olivia said, and then she turned to me. "So, Mr. Responsible? What are you doing here? Making cupcakes for your mom like last year?"

"That can't be it," Grace said. "His mom's birthday must be over by now."

"I, uh . . . kind of missed it," I said. "So I'm making her cookies—belated birthday cookies."

Olivia, Grace, and Emma looked at Jack. Their expressions were smug.

Then Lucy started to giggle. "I get it," she said. "Responsible party. Like the only fun kind of party is one that's *irresponsible*."

"Thank you, Lucy," Jack said. "I am glad someone appreciates my humor."

Responsible party . . . what?

I still didn't get it, but I would have felt dumb asking, so I changed the subject. "I am making raisin cookies," I said. "They're my mom's favorite."

Grace made a face. *"Ewww."*

"It's okay if we don't all have the same tastes, you know," Emma said.

"It's actually better that we don't," said Lucy. "If everyone liked chocolate chip best, chocolate chips would become scarce, and the price would rise."

Jack's eyebrows about jumped off his face. "Whoa! Lucy Lu!" he said. "You not only get my humor, but you're a thinker, too. How did you know that?"

"I'm not dumb, you know," said Lucy. "I just have things to do besides pay attention."

All this time, Emma had been retrieving cookie sheets, bowls, measuring spoons, and measuring cups from the cupboards and drawers. Then she went to the giant silver refrigerator for eggs and butter. From the pantry, she brought back flour, baking soda, sugar, and walnuts. Each of these she placed on the wooden countertop by the sink.

Then she turned on the oven and said, "Okay. Who wants to do what?"

"I'll measure dry ingredients," said Grace.

"I'll set up the mixer and cream the butter and eggs," said Olivia.

"Great," Emma said. "In that case, I'll grease the cookie sheets."

Eleven years as an only child had taught me many tricks, and one of them was how to make the face of a sad, sad puppy dog. I made this face now. "Uh, so I guess I'll just make my own separate batch of cookies over here," I said, and then I slumped away toward the other side of the kitchen.

"Wait a sec, Vivek," Emma said. "You guys, we're going to have plenty of cookies. Couldn't Vivek mix in the oatmeal for us? And then he could add raisins to part of the dough for his mom. Is that okay?"

"Sure," said Olivia.

"Go for it," said Jack, "provided, that is, that I still get my agreed-upon share."

"Your cookies are secure," said Emma. "Grace? What do you think?"

"Hmph," said Grace.

Meanwhile, Lucy said nothing. She was at the table by the window, setting up some project of her own. I guessed it had to do with painting, because I noticed there were brushes.

"Come on, Grace," Emma said. "It's for his *mom*, and she is having a baby."

"Hmph," Grace said again. Then she added, "Girls are not only more responsible, but they are nicer, too."

I took this to mean yes, and went to the pantry to get a box of raisins. When I came back and saw the girls hard at work, I suddenly remembered something. "Wait a sec. Is any of this about that thing that Grace asked me—?"

Before I could finish the question, laser beams

shot from the eyes of Olivia, Emma, and Grace.

Jack saw them too. "Whooey," he said. "You seem to have touched a nerve with that one, buddy."

"Never mind," I said. "I withdraw the question."

CHAPTER TWENTY-SIX

Lucy

After a whole lot of discussion—most of it too boring to listen to—the membership had decided that I should paint flowers on Hannah's card and balloons on Lance's. I wonder if that was sexist.

Note to self: Ask Olivia.

Last year when we baked cookies, it was exciting. We set off the smoke detector. There was thunder and lightning. Then the power went out.

In the end, we ate our cookies by candlelight.

Not that I care, but Vivek did look cute by candlelight.

Also last year, our "responsible party" had been Hannah and not Jack. Hannah doesn't make as many jokes as Jack, but she works harder.

This year nothing exciting happened, but you know what? In the end, there were cookies, so no complaints—as my nana would say (usually right before she finds something to complain about).

By the time the timer dinged for the last cookie sheet, the atmosphere was thick with the sweet smells of butter, sugar, and nuts.

"Do we get to actually eat any, or are they all designated for a higher purpose?" Olivia asked Emma, who was putting away the ingredients while Grace washed the dishes.

"Why are you asking me?" Emma asked.

"Because you are the boss," said Olivia.

"Oh, no," said Emma, "not anymore. I'm just normal Emma this summer. No more bossiness. I swore it off."

"Is this about that time I called you bossy?" Olivia asked.

"What if it is?" said Emma.

"Because I never said bossiness is *bad*," Olivia said.

"Yes, you did, O," I said. "I was there. What do you think of my pictures?" I held them up to be admired.

"Excellent!" said Vivek.

"Vivek—you weren't supposed to look!" said Grace.

"I promise to pretend I never saw them," said Vivek, "but the balloons look almost 3-D, and the roses are quite realistic."

"The thorns are a nice touch," Jack added.

"*Lucy!"* Grace scolded me. "The guys were never supposed to see them!"

I felt bad, but the only thing to say was, "Oops."

"I'm pretty sure oatmeal cookies induce amnesia," Jack said. "I read it in one of my textbooks."

Vivek said, "The minimum dosage is two cookies, and three is preferable." He had not taken his eyes off the cookies since they'd come out of the oven.

"Are they cool enough to eat yet, Emma?" Olivia asked.

"I am willing to risk it," Vivek said. "If I burn my mouth, it will be for science."

"Are you having a growth spurt?" Emma asked. "I'm afraid you'll spoil your dinner."

"I'll get the milk," said Grace.

A short while later, we were all eating cookies.

"Dee-licious!" Jack said. "Good work, ladies."

"Ahem," said Vivek.

"And gentleman," said Jack.

"They're certainly much better than the plastic-wrapped s'mores we get at the campfire," Vivek said.

Emma made a face. "I don't like those either."

"They've got chocolate and marshmallow," said Grace. "What is not to like?"

"You know what would be cool?" Vivek said. "If we could have cookies on Pack Trip."

"We might be able to save some," said Emma.

"They're going fast already," said Olivia. "Besides, they'd be stale by then."

"Can you make cookies over a campfire?" Vivek asked.

"I never heard of that," said Jack.

"We could probably find a recipe *if we could go online*,"

said Olivia. "But of course"—she sighed a heartbroken sigh—"thanks to Buck, we can't."

Vivek was wrapping up cookies for his mom when Jack remembered he had to be somewhere.

"Where?" Emma asked.

"Somewhere . . . ," Jack said, and then he threw out his chest and began to sing, ". . . over the rainbow, way up high. . . ."

Olivia clapped her hands over her ears. "Okay, okay, you can *go*!"

"I've got to go too," Vivek said. "We're having a cabin meeting at five."

"Hannah's probably back by now," Emma said, "but she won't be looking for us yet. Give us your key, and we'll lock up. Mrs. Arthur might not trust us, but you do, right?"

When Vivek hesitated a moment, Grace repeated, "*Right?*"

"Right!" said Vivek. "Absolutely."

"You don't mind if I take just a *few* cookies for the road, do you?" Jack asked. "After all, without a responsible party such as myself, there wouldn't be any."

"Not too many," Emma said.

With a flourish, Jack swept a handful off the cooling rack and onto a plate. Then he clicked his heels three times, saluted, and headed for the door. Vivek was right behind him.

When they were gone, I looked at Grace. "What?" she said. "Do I have oatmeal stuck in my teeth?"

"I don't think so," I said.

"Then why are you looking at me that way?" Grace asked.

"Because I've been thinking. If you don't want to break into Silver Spur Cabin, I could do it. I don't mind."

"Seriously?" Grace's eyes lit up.

"Seriously," I said.

"Thank you." She sounded relieved. "We'll have to look at the map of Boys Camp and practice the stuff I've been working on to make sure the delivery will go okay."

"Do we have time?" Lucy asked.

"Yeah," Grace said, "if we don't waste any."

"We should have thought of it before," said Olivia. "You're athletic like Grace. Plus you're a recognized hero, known far and wide for quick thinking."

"That's embarrassing," I said.

"Three cheers for Lucy!" said Olivia—which was also embarrassing, especially when they really did cheer three times: "Hip Hip Hooray! Hip Hip Hooray! Hip Hip Hooray!"

CHAPTER TWENTY-SEVEN

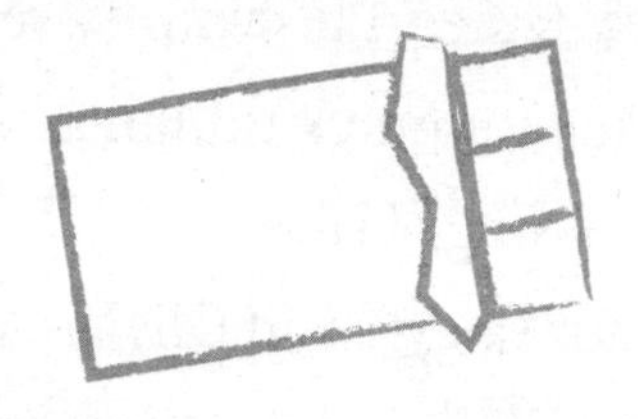

Grace

Olivia and Emma cheered for Lucy *three times*!

I cheered one and a half: "Hip Hip Hooray" and then "Hip Hip" and then nothing.

The truth is, by then I was already beginning to change my mind. If Lucy could sneak into Boys Camp and break into Silver Spur Cabin with a plate of oatmeal cookies, then so could I. Lucy had been a hero one time, but it was me who was the most coordinated, the most agile, and the strongest.

Maybe it was Snot-Nosed Grace to say so, but I liked being all those things. And I liked that people knew it, too.

On the way to breakfast the next morning, Monday, I told the membership.

"Are you sure, Grace?" Olivia asked.

"Either way," Lucy said.

"Emma?" I said.

"Pancakes," said Emma.

"What?" I said.

"Oh, sorry," said Emma. "What did you say?"

I repeated myself. Emma frowned, then shrugged. "Go for it, Grace! And it has to be tonight, right? You know that."

Now that the cookies were made, they had to be delivered fast. No one ever fell in love over stale cookies. On that the membership agreed 100 percent.

If you're looking forward to something, like acing a test, or if you're dreading something, like going to the dentist, either way, time stretches on forever.

That's how Monday was.

"Think of it like a roller coaster," Emma told me on the way back from lunch, "scary on the downhills but fun at the end when you realize you're still alive."

"Emma"—I looked at her sideways—"I know sneaking into Boys Camp won't *kill* me. The worst possible would be getting sent home by the sentries."

"A fate *worse* than death!" Olivia cried.

"And don't forget Paula will give all your stuff to charity," Emma said.

"Not helpful," I said.

"I can still go," said Lucy.

"Absolutely not," I said. "My mind is made up."

Lights-out for ten-to-elevens on weeknights is nine thirty. Since Hannah had evening riding, she didn't usually get back to Flowerpot till then or even a few minutes after. This gave Olivia time after activities to retrieve the cookies from her trunk, unwrap them, and put them on plates borrowed from the mess hall. Then she wrapped each plate in clear plastic, and Lucy put a handpainted card on top.

It had been my job to write the notes on the two cards because I have the best handwriting. We had worked hard over what to say and even (of course) argued about it. In the end we voted that simple was best, and both cards could say the same thing:

Something sweet for someone sweet.

Very truly yours,

A secret admirer

"Done," Lucy announced, once the cards were securely attached.

"Now it's all up to you, Grace," said Emma.

"And if you fail, the whole PFHL enterprise was an *enormous* waste of our time and our effort," Olivia added.

"No pressure," Lucy said.

We got ready for bed after that. To make me more nearly invisible, I had borrowed a pair of Olivia's pajamas. They were dark blue and made of silk. They were way too big for me, so I had rolled up the legs and the sleeves. With fifteen minutes left before lights-out, we had one more task to complete.

It was the one we had argued about more than any of the others.

I thought it was a crock of hooey.

Olivia thought it was brilliant.

Emma thought it couldn't hurt.

As for Lucy, the idea had come from her when we were planning. She said her mom had gone through an earth-worship phase, and she had learned some spells. As soon as Olivia heard that, she'd insisted we had to include it in PFHL. Lucy wasn't so crazy about the idea, but she went along and told us what to do.

"Did you get your supplies?" she asked now.

We all had.

Mine was a pile of salt, collected a shake at a time from the dining hall and wrapped up in a napkin, which I now placed in the middle of the floor.

Olivia's was what looked like a small pile of brown slime.

"*Ewww*—what *is* that?" I asked her.

"Flower petals," she said, "only I guess they got kind of stale."

"They'll still work," Lucy said.

"How do you know? They're disgusting," I said.

"It's the essence of the thing that matters, not its outward form," Lucy explained.

I looked Lucy in the eye. "Seriously?"

"Grace!" Olivia shook her head at me. "The time for argument is past."

Emma had a flashlight to stand in for a candle—which we never would have been allowed to have. She now placed it on the floor and switched it on. As we watched, Lucy made three piles of slime petals and put them in a line, sprinkled the salt in a heart shape around them, and turned on the flashlight. Then she said, "Which way is north?"

"Why north?" I wanted to know.

"Because of the North Star, Polaris," Lucy said, as if that explained anything.

Emma pointed, and Lucy put the flashlight on that side of the heart. Then she put a plate of cookies on either side of it.

It was getting kind of crowded on the floor.

"Okay," Lucy said, "somebody turn off the lights."

I said, "I can't believe we're doing this."

Olivia said, "I know! It's so exciting!"

"That is not what I—," I started to say.

But just then the lights went out, and in the dark Lucy spoke in a singsong voice: "Oh-h-h, great spirit of oneness that binds us together in all things. One with the minerals of the earth . . . one with the flowers of the earth . . . one with the light within and without us and with the darkness all around! Hear me and lend to these sweet confections the sweet power of passionate attraction, so that they might bind together those who receive them."

"Wow," I said, while at the same time Olivia said, "Amen!" and Emma, "Sing it, sister!"

I was hoping the next part of the ceremony would be interactive. Maybe we'd all get to mutter mumbo-jumbo sounds. In the dark with the flashlight, that might be kind of cool.

But we never got that far. Before Lucy could instruct us, there was a noise outside: Hannah was back early!

As usual, Lucy moved fastest, switching off the flashlight and shoving the cookies under our bunk bed with her foot. By the time Hannah pushed the door open, the membership had dispersed to our beds and pulled up the sheets. The salt and the flower slime were still on the floor, but Hannah wouldn't notice them in the dark.

Hannah fussed around, quietly getting ready for bed. When after a few minutes she went into the bathroom, Emma whispered, "Good luck, Grace. You can do it!"

Then Lucy and Olivia chimed in: "Good luck, Grace!"

"Thanks," I whispered, and the sound was so soft I hardly heard myself.

By this time, we had thought out, planned out, and practiced everything about PFHL.

At least I hoped we had.

This was the moment of truth.

CHAPTER TWENTY-EIGHT

Grace

Emma was our authority on all things sleep related because she had done a sleep unit during fifth-grade health. According to her, the boys of Silver Spur Cabin would be most deeply asleep around two thirty in the morning.

Without a phone, I couldn't set my alarm to vibrate to wake me up. So we had asked around until finally

Emma found a kid, Eli, in Ponderosa Cabin, who had a watch with an alarm that vibrated.

In exchange for a couple of cookies, he lent it to us.

Since there is usually something to worry about, I am not a good sleeper. That night I was not only worried about eluding the sentries; I was also worried I wouldn't wake up.

I fretted and tugged the sheets and checked the time and couldn't get comfortable . . . until what seemed like five minutes before the vibration on my wrist woke me like a buzzing bee.

"Wha . . . ?" I sat up straight, then clapped my hand over my mouth. Oh, no—had I woken Hannah?

I waited and listened, but the only sound was four girls breathing.

Quiet as a mouse, I rolled out of bed and slipped on my shoes. Quiet as a mouse, I reached under the bunk and pulled out one plate of cookies. Quiet as a mouse—one that knows how to twist a doorknob—I opened the door, slipped outside, and pulled the door closed.

Now I was on the flagstone path, breathing the cool night air. Adrenaline had woken most of my brain, and the air woke the rest. Fully awake, I was fast. I was coordinated. I was agile.

Also, I was scared to death.

Where were the sentries? How many were there? Were they really invisible and silent? What was it like if one caught you? Did he tackle you? Were there handcuffs?

Part of me said that I should have thought of all this before, and part of me said, what good would that have done?

Okay, Grace, I said to myself. *Time to do this for real. If the sentries are invisible and silent, I will be* more *invisible and silent.*

We had calculated cookie delivery to the minute. If it went as planned, I would be back in bed in Flowerpot Cabin in less than twenty minutes, mission accomplished.

With fear to spur me on, I ran lightly on my toes.

Watch out, Boys Camp. Here I come!

CHAPTER TWENTY-NINE

Emma

Grace's *"Wha . . . ?"* wasn't very loud, and after that she was quiet as a shadow getting out the door.

Still, she woke me up.

From the moment weeks before, when she got volunteered to make the PFHL delivery, I knew I had to help her out. Grace is a wonderful person, but she said it herself—she is a coward. I couldn't bear the thought of her all alone out there. Boys Camp was crawling with sentries. What if she got caught?

Meanwhile, everyone else in Flowerpot Cabin was breathing slowly and deeply, obviously sound asleep.

I didn't want Grace to know I was following her. I didn't want to interfere with her mission. I just wanted to be there in case. So I counted to twenty to give her a good head start. Then I swiveled my butt off my bunk, slipped my feet into a pair of sneakers, and tiptoed toward the door.

Crossing the room, I kicked something—the flashlight maybe? It skittered away from my toe, and I stumbled more from surprise than anything.

Olivia's dresser was closest to the door, and I bumped that before my hand found the doorknob. I'm pretty sure I didn't make any noise, but it was a relief to be outside at last.

CHAPTER THIRTY

Lucy

I wanted like anything to stay in bed. I don't even believe in romance! Besides, I had done my share when I painted the cards *and* cast the love spell.

But the membership is the closest thing I have to sisters. Different as Grace, Olivia, and Emma are from me, I love them all.

So when Emma woke me that night, clattering and

bumping her way to the door, I knew I had to follow her.

I didn't know where my shoes were, but that didn't matter. My shower shoes were next to my bed. I slid them on, crossed the room, and slipped out the door.

CHAPTER THIRTY-ONE

Olivia

The night of the cookie delivery, I slept badly.

There was the matter of the herd of rabbits stumbling through our cabin right after Grace's watch buzzed.

And then I started to worry that someone somewhere might need my help.

Was it Grace?

But I couldn't help her. I wasn't allowed. Emma didn't

want us all galumphing around Boys Camp carrying cookies. This much I knew for sure.

With the rabbits gone, it was quiet, and I rolled over only to hear a fearsome voice cry out: "Barbecue Princesses stay out of Boys Camp! No Barbecue Princess allowed!"

I knew that voice: Brianna Silverbug! How did she get in our cabin? Was she going to sabotage PFHL?

My eyelids snapped open. I would vanquish Brianna myself!

But all I saw around me was the dark. No Brianna at all.

It must have been a nightmare, I thought, and then I yawned.

Is Grace doing okay? I wondered. *How come it's quieter than usual in here?*

I rolled over again after that and must have fallen asleep.

CHAPTER THIRTY-TWO

Grace

Cookie delivery happened on a Monday. The Friday before I had gone to the camp office and asked Paula for a Moonlight Ranch registration packet. I said I needed it to give to a friend who might be interested in Moonlight Ranch. Paula wanted to know what friend. I thought fast, and I told her Shoshi Rubinstein and gave her Shoshi's address, too.

But this was a fib. The real reason I wanted the

packet was for the map of Boys Camp that's inside. I had never been to Boys Camp. No girl ever had. But by today, Monday, I had memorized the map and knew that Silver Spur Cabin was on the swimming-pool side.

I am a pretty fast runner and, based on my sprint times in PE class, I had estimated I could make it to Silver Spur Cabin in less than four minutes. If the sentries were after me, it would be faster than that.

I could never get over how many stars there were in the Arizona sky, or how brightly they shone. Until last summer, I had known about the Milky Way only from my science book and the candy bar. Now I could see it in real life, a white foggy streak against the black ink of the sky.

The moon had already set, but the skeleton shapes of the cottonwood trees stood out against the glowing stars. Along with the bats darting overhead and the hooting owls, they created a spooky atmosphere that seemed to stamp itself on my brain.

And all of it was amplified by the strangeness of what I was doing—breaking a rule! Anything seemed possible. Anything seemed likely. Once I was done delivering cookies, I might grow wings and fly over the Grand Canyon.

There is no fence around Boys Camp, but there is a wooden gate blocking the path before you get there. It's not high enough to keep anybody out. It's more like a warning label: Beware of boys!

In one move, I vaulted the gate, which creaked under my weight. Against the rhythmic, regular night sounds of birds and insects, the noise was jarring. Would it attract sentries?

Better move faster!

The path through Boys Camp was smooth and unobstructed. From the gate to Silver Spur Cabin should have been a thirty-second dash, but I made it in twenty-five.

I saw no sign of sentries, but if they were as sneaky as everybody said, that didn't prove anything. I hoped Olivia's blue pajamas, baggy and long as they were, were doing their job as invisibility cloak. If they were, then nobody could catch me—right?

That's what I told myself.

The interiors of the cabins at Moonlight Ranch are all laid out the same way: bathroom on one side, front door on the other, one window on the far side of the wall with the door, the other on the perpendicular wall. The second window was behind the desk, which was going to create a landing platform for yours truly.

Each cabin had a nameplate on the side, the letters burned into the wood like the brand on a steer. As I passed, I read them: YUCCA . . . HOBBLE STRAP . . . CONCHO . . . BLAZING STAR . . . and finally SILVER SPUR.

Counselors lock the doors overnight, but they leave the windows open and the screens down for ventilation. Emma, the boss, had made me practice climbing in through the window of Flowerpot Cabin. I hoped that practice would pay off now.

I set the plate of cookies on the ground, pressed the screen gently with my left hand, slipped my right palm under the bottom edge, and pushed up.

Yes! Flowerpot Cabin's screen was sticky, but this

one slid easily. Soon it was open wide enough that I could pick up the plate and shove it through. Then I hopped up to shift my center of gravity over the sill and pushed my head and shoulders inside.

This was it, the last moment for changing my mind.

Why not simply leave the cookies on the desk and run? If I did, I'd be back in my own bed in four minutes and safe from the sentries forever.

But that wouldn't be PFHL.

According to PFHL, the cookies had to be placed on Lance's pillow to ensure maximum effectiveness both of flour power and Lucy's spell.

So I wriggled forward and pulled up my knees till I was crouching on top of the desk, then—silently—I twisted around and put my feet on the floor.

I was in Silver Spur Cabin! I had done it!

And, no offense to the boys of the world, but the whole place smelled like sweaty socks.

Now my job was to drop off the cookies and *go*, but can you blame me for stopping five seconds to enjoy my triumph?

I had done the baddest thing a camper at Moonlight Ranch could do, sneaked into an opposite-sex cabin in the middle of the night! I was like Eve biting the apple, the patriots throwing tea into Boston harbor, Rosa Parks sitting at the front of the bus.

Grace Xi, rebel at heart, sticking it to the man.

I pursed my lips to keep from giggling.

There was a faint patch of starlight shining on the desk behind me, but otherwise Silver Spur Cabin was so dark I might as well have been blind. Even so, my job should have been easy. I just had to leave the cookies and . . .

Wait a minute.

How did I know for sure which bunk was Lance's?

All that planning. All that thinking. All that spy work . . . and we, the membership, had never asked ourselves that question!

As I stood there paralyzed, my natural-born cowardice returned.

It didn't help that whoever was in the top bunk to my right picked that moment to roll over and mutter "rrm-rrm-rrmumble."

My heart stopped. What if whoever it was really, truly woke up? What if he had to go to the bathroom? The time for thinking was past. I had to get moving *now.*

Feeling my way, I sidestepped to the head of the only single bed, which I knew was to my right. Hannah slept in the single bed in Flowerpot Cabin. So that meant Lance also slept in the single—didn't it? It made sense, but we should have found out for sure. Anyway, the single bed was obviously occupied. I could hear the sleeper breathing. Without even exhaling, I set the plate of cookies down where I estimated the pillow had to be.

Phew! I must have estimated right. If I had put the plate on someone's face, I'd definitely know it by now.

But—uh-oh!—just as I let go of the plate, the murmle-mumble boy in the top bunk made another noise.

And then . . . *OMG!*

He sat up!

I couldn't see him in the dark, but I heard sheets rustle and suddenly felt like I was being watched. In three fast moves I hopped up onto the desk, out the window, and put my feet down on the walkway.

There was only one problem, a problem I didn't notice till I was ten steps down the path.

My right foot was bare! In my hurry, I had left a shoe behind.

CHAPTER THIRTY-THREE

Vivek

At first I felt sure the intruder who came through the window was a psycho intent on murdering us all.

But then I smelled the cookies.

Oatmeal cookies.

Whoever the intruder was, she lived in Flowerpot Cabin. So, yeah, she probably was a psycho, but a murderer? Unlikely.

I was going to say, "What are you doing?" Or, "Hi;

which one are you?" Or, "You know you will get in so much trouble if you are caught in Boys Camp, right?"

But then I realized that my speaking up would wake someone, and then she'd be sent home for sure.

So I didn't say anything. I just listened to her moving around in the dark. Best I could tell, she was over by Jamil's bed. She didn't seem to be anywhere near me.

Enough time passed that finally I couldn't stand the suspense, and I sat up, hoping to see her face.

No luck. But she must have seen me move, because she gasped and then—*bump-bump-bump*—I guess she stumbled or something.

Was it Emma?

But no. As the intruder departed, the star glow caught her hair, which was straight and black.

Grace.

That was when it came to me what she had been doing in Silver Spur Cabin—the same errand she had asked me to do!

I felt a terrible pang. To make a simple cookie delivery, Grace had risked being caught by the sentries in

Boys Camp. That's how important it had been to her!

If I had just said yes and done her a favor—if I had trusted her—she wouldn't have had to take the risk.

Staring after her, I saw that the screen was still open, so I dropped off my bunk to close it. Crossing the floor, I kicked something—Grace's shoe!

In her rush to get back out the window, she must have kicked it off.

Oh, great. Because of me, Grace was not only risking the sentries to get back to Girls Camp, but she was doing it with one foot bare!

I had to do something. I had let Grace down before, and I didn't want to do it again.

CHAPTER THIRTY-FOUR

Emma

I am not a fast runner. In fact, I am a slow runner, not to mention a little bit of a klutz, which you will know if you have been paying any attention at all.

Even Lucy knows I am a klutz.

By the time I got to the Boys Camp gate, I was convinced that getting out of bed had been a mistake. It was scary out here! The air was cool enough to give me goose bumps, or maybe I had goose bumps because bats were flying all over the place, there were huge, scary big-eyed owls hooting, and the crickets were singing their hearts out.

As for tarantulas, snakes, lizards, and scorpions—they didn't come out at night, did they?

If they did, I wouldn't be able to see them on the path. What if I stepped on a huge, meaty Gila monster?

And those were just the dangers from nature. On top of them add Buck's sentries, who lurked somewhere, or everywhere. The sentries were silent and invisible, so the fact that I hadn't heard or seen any only proved they were nearby.

Besides that, where *was* Grace? She couldn't feel my moral support if she didn't know I was here for her. I thought of the famous question about the tree that falls in the forest. If nobody heard, did it actually fall?

The tree-in-the-forest question is abstract, theoretical, and philosophical. But what happened a few moments later was none of those things: I fell flat on the ground.

To be specific, I was climbing over the Boys Camp

gate and my right foot caught one of the crossbars, tripping me in midclimb, so that I flipped over the top and landed on my back with the wind knocked out of me.

If you have never had that experience, it is terrifying, like you're paralyzed and you'll never take another breath and that's it, you are done for.

I knew I wasn't done for.

One thing about being a little bit of a klutz, I have had my share of accidents, including having the wind knocked out of me. So, scary as it was, my brain expected I'd be able to breathe again if I just waited—and my brain was right. The real trouble was that my right ankle felt tingly and strange.

Then, a second later, after I'd managed to gulp the air needed to get my heart moving again, I realized I had another problem.

From somewhere not too far away, *I heard whispering!*

But it was just Grace. Right?

No—it *couldn't* be Grace! She was on a solo mission. She had no one to whisper to.

The only explanation was sentries, sentries talking

about how best to catch me! I had to get back to Girls Camp, and I had to do it now!

I rolled over onto all fours, brought my knees up under me, and tried to stand but couldn't. With weight on it, my ankle crumpled, and now it wasn't numb anymore; it was throbbing. I couldn't even crawl to safety. There was no cover on either side of the path. There was nowhere to hide.

I closed my eyes like a little kid trying to disappear and waited forlornly to be hauled off to the camp office, and then to Phoenix, and then to the airport. I wondered if they'd let me put on clothes, or if I'd have to fly back home wearing my pajamas.

CHAPTER THIRTY-FIVE

Vivek

Grace is fast, but I am faster.

Or maybe that is true only when she is half barefoot.

We were still in Boys Camp when I caught up to her next to Yucca Cabin. I didn't want to yell and attract attention, so I reached forward and touched her shoulder, causing her to look back with wide and terrified eyes. Then she recognized me and took a breath and stopped running . . . and smiled.

I guess I was better than the other likely pursuers—a sentry, or a grizzly bear, or a zombie.

We stood there for a few seconds together, catching our breath, and then she noticed I was holding her shoe.

"Thank you," she whispered, and took it.

"You're welcome," I said, "and, Grace, I'm sorry I didn't do that favor you asked. I should have trusted you."

Grace slid her foot into the shoe, then bent down and tugged the laces tight. "Apology accepted," she said, and then she looked up at me.

You know something? Grace is sort of pretty.

CHAPTER THIRTY-SIX

August 12, Friday

Dear Mom and Dad,

How are you? I am fine.

Camp continues to be an excellent learning experience. Every day I become more accomplished at horsemanship (or maybe I should call it horseWOMANship-ha-ha!), and this week I am doing leatherwork as an activity. My favorite part is beveling. I will explain what that is when I see you.

I am enclosing with this letter the blue

ribbon I won for backstroke in the camp swim competition and the blue ribbon I won for playing "Streets of Laredo" on the piano in the talent show.

Flowerpot Cabin's Chore Score continues to be perfect. Even though we have had some setbacks, we are still hoping to win the award at the Farewell Campfire.

There has been some excitement here recently because some campers broke rules. First, some girls sneaked into Boys Camp. Then another camper got caught with an electronic device. Apparently this camper has had the electronic device all summer, but it was hidden in one of her trunks. I am only mentioning these things in case you got an e-mail about them from Paula in the office.

Did you happen to get an e-mail about them from Paula in the office? Did the e-mail have any details?

I was just wondering. There is NOTHING for you to worry about.

Pack Trip begins Sunday, and we are all looking forward to it.

I miss you very much.

Love sincerely, Grace

Dear Shoshi,

OMG, you will never believe all the stuff that has happened since the last time I wrote!

First, I'm sorry about all that mail you keep getting from the Moonlight Ranch office. It is my fault. I will explain when I see you.

Second, I have a boyfriend. His name is Vivek, and he is from Pennsylvania. I think I told you about him already because last summer I thought maybe I liked him, but I didn't know if he liked me, and then at the beginning of camp I thought he liked someone else, but that was never true—he swears.

Besides that, Emma broke her ankle. She could have gone home, but she said she wanted to stay. She has to wear a cast and she can't ride her horse, so for Pack Trip she will go in the nurse's Jeep, which has AC, and the nurse lets them drink soda and eat Fritos, so part of me thinks she is actually so lucky!

How Emma broke her ankle is she was trying to help me carry out a secret middle-of-the-night cookie delivery to Boys Camp. When she got hurt, Vivek and I helped her, and while we were helping her, we made too much noise, and a counselor named Jack came out of his cabin and shined a flashlight on us exactly like a scene in a prison-escape movie.

I was so scared I thought I would die!

But Jack was nice (he is funny, too), and he sent Vivek back to bed and picked up Emma (who is not small, but Jack is strong) and carried her to Flowerpot Cabin, and Hannah gave her Tylenol because we thought her ankle was only twisted, till the next day, when it still hurt a lot and she had to go to town to get an X-ray.

Oh, and one other thing happened. On the way back to Flowerpot Cabin, a sentry almost caught us! We never saw him, but in just the kind of deep voice you'd expect a sentry to have, he yelled at us from Girls Camp: "Halt! Who goes there?"

Jack answered him: "'Tis only I, the tiniest Billy Goat Gruff! Please don't gobble me up!"

The sentry didn't bother us after that.

I couldn't sleep the rest of that night, worrying Jack would tell the camp director

I had sneaked into Boys Camp, but guess what? The next day he said if Olivia, Emma, Lucy, and I would make campfire cookies on Pack Trip, the cookies would give him amnesia and then he would have nothing to tell.

I said, "What's campfire cookies?"

Jack said, "Cookies you bake over a campfire—duh."

I said, "How do you do that?"

Jack said, "Look it up."

The other things that happened are that Jamil, who used to have a huge crush on Lucy, doesn't like her now and is acting really weird, Olivia got ten demerits for being caught with an iPad, and our big Plan to Fix Hannah's Life didn't work the way we thought—but I don't have time to add details because siesta is over and I have to mail this letter.

Love ya always, Grace

CHAPTER THIRTY-SEVEN

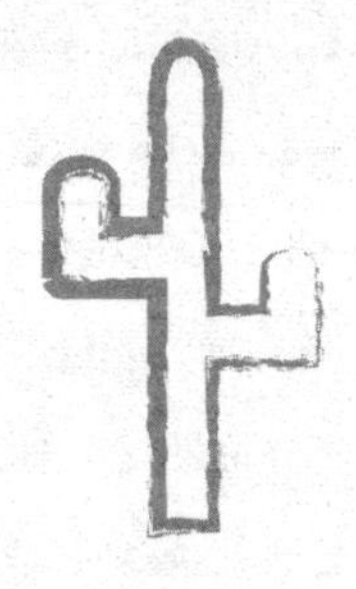

August 12, Friday

Dear Dad,

How are you?

I am fine.

I am having fun at camp. I hope you are having fun working really hard like you tell me you have to all the time.

Everything is usual here except for one strange thing that happened. Do you remember that girl Lucy from California we saw on TV that time because she killed a wolf with her bare hands? I know her now! She is a camper at Moonlight Ranch Camp too. (Did I tell you that before?)

Lucy and I have horseback riding at the same time, and she is nice, and we were friends until she did this strange thing, which was, she sneaked into my cabin when I was asleep and put cookies and a note with a picture of balloons on my pillow!

Yuck!

I don't mean the cookies were yuck. They tasted pretty good even if they didn't have any chocolate chips in them, and by a big coincidence they are Lance's (my counselor) favorite kind of cookie.

But I don't want to be anybody's boyfriend, and I told Lucy so too, but I tried to be nice about it.

Okay, gotta go swimming now. It is hot here. Is it hot there?

Love, Jamil

CHAPTER THIRTY-EIGHT

August 12, Friday

Dearest Most Esteemed Mater and Pater,

Please, please, **PLEASE**, I beg you, do not be disappointed in your one and only daughter, Olivia, who loves you very much and is very grateful for all the kind and generous things you do for her!!!

Because, the truth is, I have **SUFFERED** enough.

You already know that Buck's rule about how campers have to give up electronics has been really, really hard on me. Not only have all my friends back home ditched me (I am SURE!), but my spatial skills have deteriorated to the point that I will never pass geometry, and I have become EXPONENTIALLY more stupid without the ability to do research.

Just in case you don't know, I am not the only one at Moonlight Ranch who thinks living without a phone is basically RETURNING TO THE STONE AGE. Honestly, it is as if we each expect to encounter DINOSAURS, WOOLLY MAMMOTHS, and COVERED WAGONS on the path to North Corral, and when we don't, we are all really, really, really surprised.

So now I am going to tell you why it was IMPERATIVE that I use the iPad that I just happened to remember was still in my turquoise trunk even though I wasn't supposed to have it. And when I do tell you why, I know you will forgive me and possibly even apologize for ever getting cranky.

Here is the reason: I had to look up on Google whether it is possible to bake cookies over a campfire and also how you do it.

Spoiler alert: It is possible, and how you do it is use lots and lots of foil.

Why I had to look this up is long and complicated. One day, when I am safely grown up and you are in a really, really, really good mood, I will tell you. The important part is that we, THE MEMBERSHIP OF THE SECRET COOKIE CLUB, were helping to fix our counselor Hannah's LIFE after her stupid evil boyfriend dumped her.

In other words, it was exactly the kind of noble, generous, and selfless project you and my Sunday school teacher, Miss Oakley, are always encouraging me to undertake.

So now you cannot POSSIBLY be angry at me anymore.

Right?

I miss you and Jenny and Ralph and even

Troy, my star-athlete brother, the one you love more than me now that I got in trouble at camp and am a disgrace to the Baron family name.

Love for all eternity from your penitent daughter, Olivia

P.S. If you are wondering about the upside-down stickers, it is because I ran out of sad-faced ones and had to use happy faces.

CHAPTER THIRTY-NINE

August 13, Saturday

Dear Lucy,

I have just received your amusing letter and am writing back immediately so you will have this note before you leave camp to come home.

It tickles me that so many Moonlight Ranch traditions remain unchanged from when I was a camper there long ago. In my day, we also looked forward to Pack Trip at the end of the summer and competed vigorously for Best Chore Score and Top Cabin. We also believed there were invisible sentries silently prowling Boys Camp for girls and Girls Camp for boys. Looking back, I realize that of course the sentries were a fiction invented by Buck to keep us all behaving ourselves.

Clever Buck! The phantom sentries were probably more effective than real ones would have been, not to mention they never expected to be paid!

It also tickles me to learn you have a kooky sense of humor like your father's. Lucy, I know he hasn't been much use to you, but one day you will grow up and maybe he will, too (!). God willing, then you'll have a chance to get to know each other. Anyway, my point is that your altering your voice and calling, "Who goes there?" when you heard people coming on the path is something I can imagine him doing too.

It must have been hard for you to contain

your giggles when the answer was straight out of "Three Billy Goats Gruff."

I wonder if by now you have fessed up, or if you're going to let your bunkmates think they really encountered one of the dreaded sentries. If the latter, you are perpetuating Buck's myth, you know!

As for the failure of your matchmaking scheme, have you ever heard of a line of poetry written more than two hundred years ago by a Scot named Robert Burns? According to it, "The best laid schemes o' mice and men often go awry."

In other words, plan all you want and things still may not work out. You girls seem to have found the truth in this. I'm glad to hear that even without a new romance, she (Hannah is her name, right?) has cheered up after being so down in the dumps. Maybe she has come around to the view that boys aren't everything.

Like you, I'm surprised your mother's love spell didn't work. If anything, she seems to have too much success with them. Has she told you how it is going with the Arizona highway patrolman she met when she drove you to camp? He sounded like a decent fellow, and at least he has a steady job.

Change of topic: Things are fine here in beautiful Santa Barbara. Unlike where you are, we have ocean breezes to mitigate the summer heat. Maybe sometime before school starts, you can come here for a visit? If those triplets you watch can spare you, that is. I bet they and their mother miss you desperately!

Hope to see you soon, and lots of love,

Aunt Freda

CHAPTER FORTY

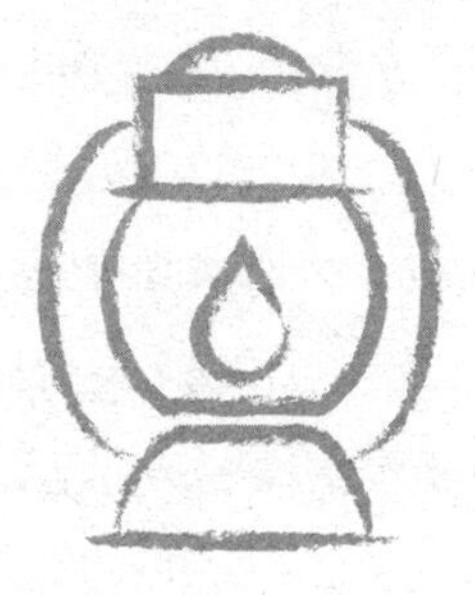

(From the Moonlight Ranch Handbook for Families)

The culmination of summer activities is the annual Pack Trip, which promotes self-sufficiency in a natural outdoor setting, teaches valuable camping skills, and encourages appreciation of the power and beauty of the rugged Southwestern environment.

With their gear packed on their horses, campers ride beyond the boundaries of Moonlight Ranch to scenic Ocotillo Lookout, a promontory with a panoramic view of the vast Arizona landscape. The approximately four-hour trail ride gives campers the chance to utilize, consolidate, and reflect upon the equestrian progress they have made during the course of the summer program.

As with all Moonlight Ranch activities, appropriate breaks for hydration and allergen-free nutrition are built into the travel schedule, and campers are consistently supervised by well-trained and caring professional staff.

Upon arrival at Ocotillo Lookout, campers grouped according to cabin assignment set up their own outdoor kitchens and sleeping areas. This unique opportunity to customize accommodations enables each group to practice teamwork and to explore and realize their own potential for enterprise, creativity, and ingenuity.

During their stay at Ocotillo Lookout, campers cook and clean for themselves in addition to caring for their horses. At the same time, they have the opportunity to enjoy a curtailed schedule of educational and recreational activities, including athletic competitions, nature hikes, trail rides, and singalongs.

All in all, it's easy to see why campers and counselors alike call Pack Trip a highlight of the summer.

Special note: In past years, some parents have expressed concern over the necessarily primitive nature of "bathroom" facilities during Pack Trip. Road access at the Ocotillo Lookout property is limited to passenger vehicles, and plumbing is nonexistent. For this reason, we must rely on time-honored strategies for waste processing and disposal. Of course, our methods are fully compliant with established best practices for hygiene, water quality, and the natural environment as outlined by the United States Bureau of Land Management (Publication No. 16-2783).

Most campers become comfortable with our old-fashioned arrangements as a matter of necessity. Please feel free to call Paula in the Moonlight Ranch office should you wish to discuss the particular needs of your camper.

CHAPTER FORTY-ONE

Lucy

Before Hannah caught Olivia with the iPad and confiscated it because she had to or she would lose her job and there were tears on both sides and drama on Olivia's side only, Olivia had the presence of mind to copy out the campfire cookie recipe she had found online.

But perhaps you have heard of a line in a poem by an old poet named Scot. It goes: "The best laid recipes of mice and man often get messed up."

Perhaps Scot had tried making campfire cookies for himself.

Believe me, there are many possibilities for mess-ups, something I know because we experienced every single one during Pack Trip.

How you make campfire cookies is make normal cookie dough, then build a miniature oven in the shape of a hollow cube out of at least six layers of aluminum foil, drop cookie dough on the bottom of the oven, fold the foil over the top to seal it, and put the whole thing on a grill on top of a campfire.

Here is what will happen: You will burn the bottoms of lots of cookies, and lots more will stick so you have to eat them together with foil or not at all.

After a while, the foil will tear, and bits of dough will fall into the fire, where they will smoke for a long time before finally flames shoot up and they become charcoal briquettes. After this, you will raise the oven farther from the fire, and then your cookies will first be raw and later be dried out and hard as hockey pucks.

You will fight with all your friends and blame each other.

And you will feel stupid! Because you are the Secret Cookie Club! And if you can't even bake an edible cookie, what good are you?

CHAPTER FORTY-TWO

Emma

If there is a world's record for amount of cookie dough wasted in three days, we probably broke it during Pack Trip.

I felt really guilty about this. With some of my friends at home, I volunteer at a food bank, and I know there are hungry people in this world. What kind of sense did it make to literally incinerate ingredients in, over, and around a campfire?

I said this to Grace on Tuesday afternoon. It was our

last day at Ocotillo Lookout, and we were still trying to get the baking right.

Ocotillo Lookout is a mesa (not a butte!) that rises about one thousand feet off the desert floor. Because the country around it is rugged, flat, and treeless, you look out to the cloud-studded blue forever in all directions. It's like being a speck on top of the world.

There is no natural cover at Ocotillo Lookout, so the first thing we did when we got here was help the counselors erect blue tarp canopies. These were to protect us from sun during the day and from thunderstorms overnight. Luckily, the nighttime weather stayed clear, so we got to sleep out under the stars.

At mealtimes, we sat on the ground or on rocks or benches we made ourselves out of whatever wood we could scavenge. I won't tell you about the bathrooms because, short version, there weren't any. We cleaned up with wet wipes or water from jugs brought in on a dirt road by truck. As for the other bathroom-type functions, I'll just say shovels were involved, and it was all very environmental.

By the fourth afternoon, my clothes were dusty, and I smelled like campfire smoke. I was sweaty from the heat and tired from sleeping poorly on the ground.

And I was happy.

Olivia, Lucy, Grace, and I had fought till we were so sick of fighting there was nothing left but to be friends again, and now—at last—we were.

Also, I hope it's not braggy to say so, but I was proud of the really sweet little outdoor kitchen we had set up for ourselves. Our utensils came from Mrs. Arthur back at camp and included a cutting board, pots, knives, bowls, plates, and napkins. Grace had found a forked stick and stuck it in the ground, and we had hung a ladle from it.

We didn't actually need a ladle, but the setup looked really cool.

Each kitchen had a cooler for perishable food. The truck brought us ice, too. Anytime I felt like I was some kind of pioneer woman roughing it on the Oregon Trail, I reminded myself that the pioneers didn't get ice deliveries.

In case you haven't guessed, by this time I had taken

back my vow not to be in charge. It was me that organized the kitchen, or more accurately, me that told Grace, Emma, and Lucy how they should organize the kitchen. With my broken ankle, I wasn't good for much besides ordering other people around. Also, I could see that if I let anyone else be in charge, we wouldn't get the kitchen organized till Pack Trip was over.

The prep area was the cooler, which we placed in the center of the space we had mapped out. The campfire was in one corner, and the cleanup area (a plastic tub with a sponge and a rag) opposite. We even had a flowering cactus centerpiece on a table we made out of rocks and boards.

Hannah helped too, but she emphasized that it was our kitchen, and we should be in charge. Same with the cookies, which is probably one reason we wasted so much dough.

"If we think of it as experimenting instead of baking," Grace said, "we'll feel better. The rules are different. Some stuff has to get used up."

"Is that true?" I was dropping spoonfuls of dough onto

greased foil for what had to be the zillionth time. If we were going to fulfill our promise to Jack, this batch had to work. We didn't have time or ingredients to make another one.

"Absolutely," Grace said. "I mean, my parents are scientists, and they do experiments. In the end it's worth the waste if you learn something or get something good. Ready?"

"Ready," I said. One thing about foil ovens, they're flimsy. Now Grace pinched two lower corners in her fingers and I pinched the opposite corners, and we moved the oven from the prep area to the grill above the campfire. As always, the dough shifted and the sides drooped in transit, but when at last the oven was safely in place, I felt optimistic.

And what do you know, this batch worked!

Lucy and Olivia had been on a wildflower walk. With my broken ankle, I couldn't go, and Hannah had given Grace permission to stay back with me. By the time Lucy and Olivia returned, we were transferring golden-brown cookies to a cooling rack made out of crisscrossed manzanita twigs—Grace's idea.

Lured by the aroma, a small crowd came over to see how things were going. We had marked off our kitchen with a border of rocks and branches laid out on the ground. There was nothing to keep people from stepping over it, but no one did. Instead, they lined up and watched as if we had a cooking show or something.

"How many good ones ya got this time?" asked Angela, a seven-eight-nine from Primrose Cabin.

"Thirty-six, so far," I said, "and I'm really sorry, but you can't test one."

"Yesterday you let me test one," said Brendan, also a seven-eight-nine.

"Because it was half burned," Grace explained. "None of this batch burned, and we have to save them to share at the campfire later on."

Walking by, Jack must have heard this, because he made an abrupt course change and came over to join the spectators. "Is that a promise?" Wearing his trademark old-man hat along with a pink Hawaiian shirt, red cargo shorts, and flip-flops, he looked out of place as usual in the sea of denim, plaid, and Western boots.

"'Cause if it's not," he went on, "I think my memory of certain, shall we say, *transgressions,* might be more vivid than I thought."

I gulped. He meant he might remember about Grace and me in Boys Camp. But he wouldn't tell Buck, would he?

Olivia said, "It's absolutely a promise. Don't you worry."

Brendan said, "What's a 'grans-teshun'?"

"A *sin,*" said Jack, and then he waggled his fingers and bugged out his eyes. This made Brendan and Angela giggle, but he wasn't looking at Brendan and Angela. At first I thought he was looking at me, but then I realized it was actually something over my shoulder

And then the something over my shoulder giggled too.

I turned around and saw . . . Hannah. Her eyes were bright, and so was her smile. She was looking straight at Jack.

O . . . M . . . G.

CHAPTER FORTY-THREE

Grace

OMG!

CHAPTER FORTY-FOUR

Olivia

OMG!

CHAPTER FORTY-FIVE

Lucy

Wait, what?

CHAPTER FORTY-SIX

Brianna Silverbug

Olivia Baron and I both had afternoon riding, and all summer long I had wanted to ask her a question. Now almost everyone in the whole camp was riding back from Pack Trip—creating a cloud of red dust as we went—and she was ahead of me on the trail. As usual, she was mumbling something—talking to her horse?—but I couldn't hear what she was saying.

I grinned and shook my head and wished for the

millionth time I had my phone. If I had, I would have put a video of Olivia riding Shorty up on YouTube. The tall, glamorous black girl and the stubby, mousy horse were what my mom would call one odd couple for sure.

We were more than halfway back to camp and, maybe because I didn't sleep well on the ground, my mind was wandering aimlessly. It was as if I didn't have the energy either for conversation or for focusing on any single thing.

The day was cloudy, unusual in the desert, and Jane had told us there might be a storm overnight. Pack Trip had been fun, but I hated being dirty. The Flowerpot girls were our Chore Score archrivals, but they sure made delicious cookies.

We had been riding single file on a trail, but now the trail veered right and fed into a dirt road, the same road used by the nurse's car and the truck that brought supplies for Pack Trip.

On the road, there was room for me to ride next to Olivia. This was the last day we'd be on horseback and probably my best opportunity to ask my question. I hesitated. Everybody knew Olivia Baron was the most stuck-up girl at camp. If I spoke to her, she'd probably look down her nose as usual.

But, oh heck—who cared if she did? Camp was almost over. I might never even see her again. Besides, I was really, really, *really* curious.

I bumped my horse's flanks with my heels and clicked my tongue to urge her forward. Sheba is a purebred quarter horse, only five years old, and lively. Even so, she didn't catch Shorty right away. Only after a couple of minutes did I recognize the significance of this. Shorty wasn't poky anymore.

Now I really wanted to ask my question, so I goaded Sheba into a trot—even though I knew we weren't supposed to. Sure enough, Cal, the counselor in charge of the horses, hollered at me, "Don't trot that horse!"

"Sorry!" I called back, but mission accomplished. I was now riding next to Olivia. When I looked over at her, I realized she wouldn't be looking down her nose at all, not even if she wanted to. Shorty was so short that for the first and only time ever, my view was the top of Olivia's white hat.

"Hey," I said. "How ya doin', Olivia? Those were really great cookies you guys made."

"Thank you," said Olivia.

I noticed she had her braids tucked up under her hat and she was wearing a pink bandanna (so was I) with a plaid, Western-style short-sleeve shirt (so was almost everybody). The shirt was mostly magenta and turquoise, the most popular colors that year. Unlike me, she looked clean. In fact, somehow Olivia almost always managed to look better than the rest of us girls.

I was trying to think of a lead-in to my question when Olivia surprised me. "Uh, Brianna?" she said. "Can I ask you something?"

"Oh, that's funny," I said. "I wanted to ask you something too."

"You can go first if you want," Olivia said.

"Oka-a-ay, so, well . . . what I want to know is, what is it you say to Shorty, anyway?" I asked. "I mean, he's so different from how he was at the beginning of camp. He was a poke-along, and now he walks faster than Sheba. The first time I saw him, I thought of Eeyore—you know, from *Winnie-the-Pooh*?"

"He reminded me of Eeyore too!" Olivia said.

"I like Eeyore," I said.

"Yeah, as a character, but not to ride," Olivia said.

"Yeah, no," I said. "Definitely not to ride. So what is it you say to Shorty? Is that why he's different?"

"Maybe," Olivia said. "But I don't say anything that special. I just give him pep talks, you know? Like I tell him, 'Lift and step! Lift and step! You can do it, Shorty! You're a handsome horse!'" She shrugged. "Do you think he has started to believe it?"

"Definitely," I said. "What is it you wanted to ask me?"

"Oh, nothing," she said. "Forget it."

Now I was curious again. "No, really. Ask away."

"Okay, if you say so, here goes: Why did you call me 'Barbecue Princess' last year? I never said anything bad about you."

"I didn't!" I said.

"Yeah, you did. That girl Quintana in your cabin told me."

"Quintana?" I repeated. "She was *always* spreading stories about people! Didn't you know that? She just liked to stir up trouble!"

"So you really never said that?" Olivia said. "'Cause I hate it when people say stuff like that."

The Moonlight Ranch main gate came into view in the distance. We would be back in twenty minutes—maybe fifteen. All the horses sensed that the barn was near, and they picked up the pace.

"Olivia," I said, "I don't think I ever called you Barbecue Princess. But even if somebody did—it's better than being a dust-mop duchess, right?"

Olivia laughed. "I'd have to think about that," she said.

CHAPTER FORTY-SEVEN

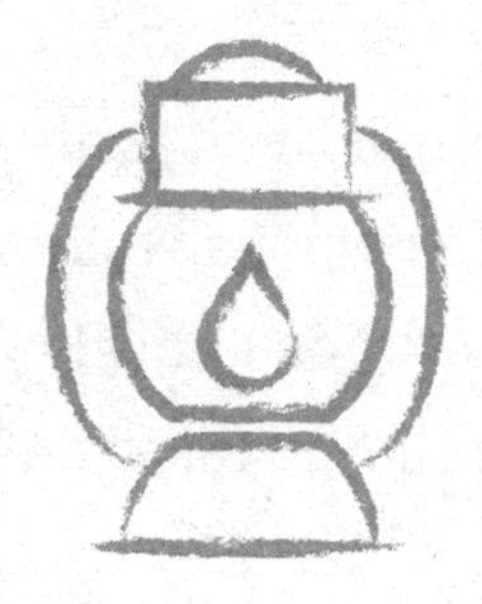

Vivek

From Grace I learned that the campers in Flowerpot Cabin think of themselves as "the membership" because they are all members of a cookie club.

"Aha!" I said. "So that proves it was the four of you who mailed me boxes of cookies last year!"

"I can't tell you *that*, Vivek," Grace said. "It's a secret."

I sighed and said, "Of course it is," because here is something I just learned about girls: The very idea of secrets thrills them.

Why is that, do you think? And is it true of all girls, or only certain ones?

I will ask my mom. If I do it soon, she will answer me. But if I wait till after the baby comes, she will probably say, "Please, Vivek. You know I have no time for silly questions. I have a baby to take care of!"

Everyone tells me I will love being a big brother, but I am not convinced.

That, however, is a worry for later—when I am home again in Pennsylvania. For one more day, I am still at camp, and I have a different worry. I need to tell Grace that we are breaking up.

Please do not hate me for this. Grace is a very nice girl. She can do almost anything and do it well. She is pretty.

But I am not ready for the responsibilities of being a boyfriend. Here is what I mean. Last year I gave Grace a small present at the end of camp because I wanted to. This year it is different. She *expects* me to give her a present at the end of camp! She told me she already has one for me.

Too much pressure!

Right away I became anxious about finding the right

present for her. This is not easy when the only place to obtain a present is the Moonlight Ranch Trading Post, and the only things sold in the camp store are postcards and chips and candy and Oreos.

I do not need this anxiety. And so I will have to break up with Grace. In fact, for now I think I will give up on all girls altogether.

That said, I must in fairness praise the girls of Flowerpot Cabin for one particular accomplishment. The four of them worked very hard to perfect their method for baking campfire cookies, and in the end they succeeded. The ones we ate around the campfire at Ocotillo Lookout on the last night of Pack Trip were perfection in cookie form.

Jack pronounced them scrumptious, then said, "Wait a minute. I could be wrong, but I think I'm forgetting something. No girls I know ever sneaked into Boys Camp, did they? No? I thought not."

Hannah, the Flowerpot counselor, was sitting beside him, and giggled. I have noticed that many of his comments make her giggle. He is a funny guy.

CHAPTER FORTY-EIGHT

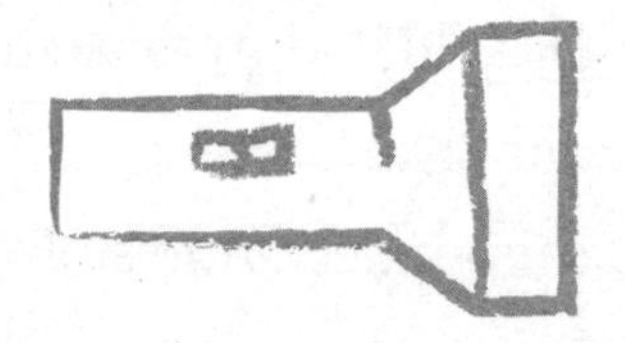

As always, Buck announced the Moonlight Awards at the Farewell Campfire on the last night of camp.

Silver Spur won Chore Score.

And Purple Sage was Top Cabin.

Brianna, Kate, Maria, and Haley—the girls of Purple Sage Cabin—whooped and squealed when the name was called. Lucy whooped and squealed too, then remembered this was Flowerpot's archnemesis and toned it down to polite applause.

"Hooray for Jane!" Hannah hollered generously. She had been in an especially good mood ever since Pack Trip.

"At least they didn't win Chore Score too," Grace whispered.

In fact, the Secret Cookie Club membership had known for a while they couldn't win Top Cabin. The demerits Olivia got when she was caught with an electronic device had knocked them out of contention.

The Chore Score competition, on the other hand, had gone down to the wire. Two nights before, a storm had swept through, knocking out power for several hours. At breakfast yesterday, there were no pancakes for Emma, no hot food at all.

And during cleanup, there was no power for the Dandy Dust Mop. The Purple Sage girls, accustomed after eight weeks of camp to using it, had allowed their hand-mopping skills to deteriorate. They lost five points for their dirt-streaked floor, putting them just behind

Silver Spur Cabin, which had lost two points earlier in the summer for cookie crumbs on the walkway outside.

As of yesterday, Flowerpot had the only perfect Chore Score at camp. The award was in the bag, right?

Wrong.

Because that very day after breakfast, they made a critical mistake. Other than a quick poke with the broom to kill off obvious dust bunnies, no one had looked under the bunk beds. On inspection duty that day, Annie, the head counselor, did look, and what she saw horrified her—ants by the zillion marching from the wall to Grace's suitcase, where, one cookie molecule at a time, they were laying waste to her hidden stash of Oreos.

Flowerpot got zeros in overall tidiness, surfaces, and beds—a devastating loss of fifteen points. In the comment section, Annie wrote only, "Ewww!"

The wake-up bell rang at six forty-five, as usual, on the last day of camp. Parents were due to arrive around lunchtime. When the campers were gone, there would be a farewell dinner for counselors. Hannah had a reservation to fly from Phoenix to New York City the following day.

For Hannah, there had been many sad days this summer and many long days, too. She and Lance, the handsome counselor from Silver Spur Cabin, had flirted under the stars after evening riding, but in the end she realized she was only a sounding board for his complaints about his ex-girlfriend.

Some days she had felt worthless. But her campers got her through—their goofiness, their schemes, and most of all, their affection. They thought she was worth something, and maybe they were right.

And then, like a gift, she had realized that this unlikely guy named Jack was interested in her, and she found to her surprise that she was interested back. Hannah hated the word "relationship" because it was lame, and she hated the word "romance" because it sounded like something at the drugstore next to the cheap perfume. So she and Jack had a "thing," dimensions to be defined later . . . when he had returned to Chicago and she was back home on Long Island.

And here it was the last morning, and all of a sudden an eventful summer was wrapping up in a feverish blur of packing.

Even after dealing with the ant infestation, Grace still finished first. Olivia was having a hard time closing her trunk. Emma kept offering good advice on packing to Lucy, who had borrowed two duffel bags from the camp lost and found since the latches on her footlocker were broken.

"Hey, Grace," Olivia said. "So, are Vivek's parents coming to get him? Or just his dad?"

"How should I know?" Grace said.

Everybody stopped what they were doing and looked at Grace, who looked back. "What? Oh—I guess I forgot to tell you. After the campfire last night, we broke up."

Olivia rushed across the bunkroom and put her arms around her friend. "Oh, you poor, poor, poor, poor, poor, poor *thing*! Tell me, is your heart entirely shattered? I never liked him! He isn't worth the nail on your pinky toe!"

"I didn't say he broke up with me," Grace said.

"Did he?" Emma asked.

"Kind of," Grace admitted. "But in the end it was on both sides. He's cute to look at, but not really boyfriend material."

"Sounds like Lance," Hannah said. "Jack, on the other hand, gave me cookies."

Once again, the girls looked at one another. Finally Emma spoke up. "Hannah, I hope this is not a big deal. But actually, Jack didn't. *We* put the plate of cookies on your pillow. We wanted you to think they were from Lance."

Hannah laughed. "Not those cookies. I knew *those* cookies were from you. As if I wouldn't recognize a Lucy Ambrose original watercolor! But Jack brought me some of those snowball cookies right out of the oven. They really cheered me up too. He's a guy who appreciates flour power."

"That's right," Emma recalled. "A couple of weeks ago when we baked cookies, he left all of a sudden. It was Vivek who locked up the kitchen."

"He said he was going over the rainbow," Lucy remembered.

"That's *so* sweet!" said Olivia. "But while we're on the

subject of everybody's love life, there's one more thing I don't get. Lucy, what is with you and Jamil?"

Facing away from the others, Lucy didn't answer. She was trying to unstick the zipper on one of the borrowed duffel bags.

"Lucy!" everyone chorused, and finally she looked up.

"Jamil?" she said. "Oh, him. He tried to break up with me too, a couple of weeks ago, right after Emma broke her ankle. And I told him he couldn't because we weren't going together. Or if we were, he should have told me first. Then he said something about cookies I didn't understand, and I got worried that he might be even crazier than the average boy, and I walked away, and he hasn't spoken to me since."

"Oh, you *poor, poor* thing!" Olivia said. "And now is your heart shattered?"

"It is," Lucy admitted. "But not about that. I really wish we had won Chore Score."

"Next summer we will," Olivia said.

"Next summer!" Grace and Emma agreed.

Then all four of them looked at Hannah, and Hannah

hesitated. "That's pretty far in the future to plan, don't you think?" she said. "A lot could happen between now and then."

"Well, *duh.* But you can't let that stop you," Olivia said.

"It didn't stop us," Grace said.

"Nothing went like we thought, but that was okay," Emma said. "I mean, my cast comes off in two weeks."

"I hope I can come back next year," Lucy said, "but I'll miss you guys in between."

"I have an idea," said Grace. "We could bake cookies and send them to each other during the year."

"Very original," said Hannah. "Can I get in on it? After all, you're using my grandfather's recipes."

"Sure you can," said Emma, "if you promise to come back next summer too."

Hannah thought of what she had missed out on this year. The marble-lined corridors, the air-conditioning, the ancient art and high heels. Then she looked out the window at the bright blue sky and looked down into the faces of her girls.

"Oh, why not?" she said. "Next summer! And the other cabins better watch out."

Cookie Recipes

Here's some good advice from
Hannah's grandfather about baking.

1) Read the recipe through before you get to work.

2) Next, get out ingredients, utensils, bowls, and pans so you know you have everything you need.

3) Finally, prepare each item so that it's in the state described in the ingredient list. In the s'mores cookie recipe, for example, melt the butter and pulverize the graham crackers before you preheat the oven. Remember to ask an adult for help with the oven or mixer.

S'mores Bar Cookies

These are much better than the Marshmallow Fluff version prepared at Moonlight Ranch.

(Makes 24 bar cookies)

1 cup melted butter

4 cups graham cracker crumbs

12 ounces (2 cups) chocolate chips (milk chocolate or semisweet)

2 cups miniature marshmallows

Preheat oven to 350°F. Grease a 13-by-9-inch baking pan with either butter or cooking spray.

In a medium bowl, mix butter and cracker crumbs. Press half this mixture into the bottom of the prepared pan. Sprinkle with chocolate chips and marshmallows. Top with remaining butter-cracker mixture. Bake 15 minutes.

These are easiest to cut if they are completely cool. Consider refrigerating for a few minutes if you are in a hurry.

Campfire Cookie Method

Use your favorite sturdy cookie dough recipe, store-bought cookie dough, or the oatmeal cookie recipe below.

The secret to successful campfire cookies is a successful campfire made with a grownup's help. This means your fire should have burned for a while so that the briquettes or wood are glowing but no longer producing flames. There should be a grate of some kind over the fire, approximately six inches above it.

Place a piece of aluminum foil on a griddle or a very sturdy cookie sheet suitable for camping (meaning not the nicest one in the kitchen). Grease the foil, either with cooking spray or butter. Drop the cookie dough by generous teaspoons onto the foil. Allow a two-inch space between the future cookies.

Now you build the oven by tenting an oversize second piece of foil over the griddle, allowing about four inches of space above and around the cookies so air can circulate. Crimp the upper and lower edges together loosely.

Wearing fire gloves or similar protection, set the griddle or skillet with its foil oven on the grate over the campfire.

After 3 or 4 minutes, lift an edge of the foil with tongs so you can see how the cookies are doing. You may need to adjust the height of the grate if the bottoms of the cookies are burning, or you can try removing some coals. It takes practice! Depending on your fire and the dough, the cookies should be done in 7 to 10 minutes.

Chewy Oatmeal Cookies

With added raisins, these are Vivek's mom's favorites.

(Makes 36 cookies)

1 ½ cups flour

½ teaspoon salt

½ teaspoon baking powder

1 cup butter, softened

1 cup brown sugar (light or dark)

1 cup white sugar

2 eggs

3 cups old-fashioned rolled oats

1½ cups raisins, chocolate chips, or a combination (optional)

Heat oven to 350°F. Grease cookie sheets with either cooking spray or butter, or use parchment paper as a liner.

Thoroughly combine flour, salt, and baking powder in a medium bowl.

In an electric mixer, beat butter and both sugars until light and fluffy. Add eggs one at a time and mix until just combined.

With the mixer on low speed, add the dry ingredients slowly and mix until combined. Then mix in remaining ingredients. Do not overmix.

Using about a tablespoon each, roll dough into balls and place about two inches apart on prepared cookie sheet.

Bake for about 12 to 15 minutes or until brown around the edges. Let cookies cool for a few minutes on the cookie sheet before transferring to a rack to cool to room temperature.